HELLFIRE TO COME

MAYA DANIELS

By Maya Daniels

Infernal Regions for the Unprepared

Vinci Books

vinci-books.com

Published by Vinci Books Ltd in 2025

1

The publisher and the author have made every effort to obtain permissions for any third party material used in this book and to comply with copyright law. Any queries in this respect should be brought to the attention of the publisher and any omissions will be corrected in future editions.

A CIP catalogue record for this book is available from the British Library.

Paperback ISBN: 9781036706647

Chapter One

BROOKLYN

All I needed was to take one more breath.

"A breath is the genesis of existence," I murmured, detached, as my thumb traced slow, aimless circles over my knee, somehow anchoring me to a reality I could scarcely recognize. It felt as though I would unravel completely, dissipate into oblivion, the moment that minimal contact ceased.

How did everything go so wrong, so fast? If I thought I was unprepared for the things that happened until this very moment, I sure as all hells was unprepared for the new inferno barreling toward me, ready to destroy me once and for all.

I needed to turn the helplessness I felt into anger so I could think, so I could go kill everyone who dared take my friend. Instead, here I was, like a tumbleweed rolling aimlessly through time and space with no certain destination in mind while shivers raked my frame at the most random intervals.

The tremor I felt in my bones was not fear, however, it was the echo of a soul on the brink of disintegration, haunted by the certainty that stillness meant vanishing. Because what good was I to anyone if all they did was pay for being near me.

So, with each breath, I tried to believe: believe in the lie that breath is a sacred link to my friend, a living thread connecting soul to soul, self to the universe. I rubbed at the soiled fabric of my pants again, each stroke a futile prayer to know that Alice was okay. That she was not broken the way I was. The way they broke me.

"Breath is life," I commanded myself, hollow and stern, exhaling sharply until my breath clung to the mirror before me in a fragile fog. I'd stared into that mirror for days, after each empty-handed search for my friend, willing it to tell me where she was. Instead of answering, the mist warped my reflection into something grotesque, demonic, a visual echo of the emptiness clawing at my insides. A true picture of what I was.

Failure. Useless. Helpless.

A monster, just like those hurting Alice while I stared at myself doing nothing.

I could not find myself in the distorted reflection, nor could I find Alice anywhere in the city. The tether was severed, no matter how hard I reached or pleaded for a sign that she was near. So how could breath claim to be a bridge when I felt marooned?

If breath truly belonged to life, why did each inhale feel like erosion, like another layer of my being was flaking and drifting away, brittle as dried leaves crushed under a brutal heel?

And yet, all that remained of me was that motion. That breath was the only connection to my friend. Just one more, I urged myself. Perhaps, if I could summon another inhale, another fleeting act of will, I might wake, return to the moment before my world shattered.

"Let it be a dream," I pleaded. A nightmare, more truthfully. But still… a dream.

Because I couldn't look reality in the eye. I couldn't accept that she'd just recovered from my brutal attack only to be thrown to the wolves who were ready to rip her to pieces, not without it tearing the last shred of sanity from my grasp. I couldn't accept that Alice was gone, taken, ripped away because someone among us was a disgrace, a traitor. Because if I admitted that truth, I'd have to admit the rawest one of all: I failed her. As a guardian. As a friend. As a supposed protector of those I swore to keep safe.

Worse still…

I failed her as family.

And Alice was my family. She and Dominic were the only real family I had left.

That truth dropped inside me like lead into water, dragging with it my soul toward the gaping, cursed earth beneath me, eager to swallow my hollow shell whole. She wasn't just another person with some invested interest in me. She was real. The one who saw me at my most pathetic —stripped of power, dignity, even hope—and didn't flinch. She stood there when I was a mindless monster, believing in me when I didn't believe in myself. She never turned away from me. Not once. She risked her fragile mortal flesh so she could stand by my side with no questions asked regardless of her safety because, as she said, "that's what friends do."

She meant more to me than Veronica ever did. Just one more revelation stabbing like a nail in the coffin the Council was custom building for me. And what good did that do her? What good did I do her?

All the power I carried, all the damned gifts bestowed

upon me from bloodlines…what were they worth if I couldn't even shield her from the very monsters hunting my own dreams? Monsters that now walked freely while she paid with her human life for my mistakes.

Alice is not a human, the voice hissed in the back of my skull, sharp, sudden, enough to jolt my heart like a defibrillator.

No. She wasn't human.

And that's why she was taken. Why she was suffering somewhere beyond my reach. And all I could do was sit there, staring at a reflection that barely looked alive, while the universe ground on in a cruel, indifferent silence.

"Brooklyn?"

A whisper, almost lost in the hush between heartbeats was followed by the softest knock, a ghost's caress against the polished wood. The voice as well was just a fracture in the silence, a desperate murmur from the only soul who dared reach for mine through the thundering of chaos within my being. My mate's low voice trembled, not from anger, but from knowing. Knowing that the fortress I'd built from grief and guilt wasn't made of stone but of glass, and still, he knocked, aching to be let in even though recognizing the price he would need to pay may be steep.

Dominic wasn't merely asking to cross a door's boundary, however. No, he was begging to step into the wreckage I had become, into the shadows and sorrow I wore like rusted armor, jagged and cruel. Armor I forged from despair, lined with the blades of my own guilt, and I knew, if he stepped too close, it would make him bleed.

And I… I was terrified of what he'd find inside.

So, I did what cowards do. I retreated further into the hollow shape of myself, sinking into the chair as if it might swallow me whole. I feigned absence, as though I were still out there, wandering the world for a friend I'd already lost to the night.

But Dominic knew. Sometimes I thought he knew me better than I knew myself.

He could hear my heartbeat, a mournful echo trembling beneath ribs heavy with grief, the same way I could feel his, a quiet drum of love and defiance through the silence we both drowned in.

"Let me in, my love, it's been days where you suffer alone." His voice cracked beneath the weight of desperation, fragile as butterfly wings, trembling with the ache of a man begging to hold together in me what was already unraveling. "You don't need to carry this guilt, Brooklyn. Let me help you search. We'll find her faster together."

But we both knew the truth. I didn't want help. Not anymore. I had opened my soul, piece by fragile piece, to the idea that I could lean on others. That maybe, just maybe, I didn't have to fight this battle alone. And look where that tender foolishness led me.

Look what it cost.

I'd learned the hard way that trust is a currency too often forged and too easily broken. I betrayed my own instincts when I chose to trust.

Now, Alice, the one person apart from Dominic I couldn't afford to lose, might pay the price for my hope.

A single misstep of faith, and it may have signed her death warrant.

"Go away, Dominic." My voice cracked like a brittle shell beneath an unassuming foot, and I tore myself from the mirror's accusing gaze. I paced the room in jagged, restless strides, every stomp a battle cry against the ache in my chest. "I'm not fit for company."

"I don't need company," he replied immediately, calm and unwavering. "I need you."

A bitter laugh escaped me, hollow and sharp. "We all need things, Dominic. But want doesn't shape reality. It just burns in our bones when the world denies us the simplest of things."

The silence that followed was agonizing. I heard him shift, his boot rasping across the wooden floor as he recoiled from my cruelty. The stories he'd shared with me about losing his family, the grotesque way the Council punished everything he held dear hung between us. Guilt swelled in my throat, but I swallowed it like poison.

"You think driving us away is helping Alice?" His voice trembled, not with anger but with pain. "You think pushing me away is what she would want?"

There was a muffled thump as his fist met the wall beside the door, a muted echo of the storm within him. My instincts flared, snapping my head toward the sound. I wanted to snarl, to fight, to retreat deeper into the grief that cloaked me, but he kept going.

"We all love her. We all want her back."

I stormed to the door, my hand wrapping around the knob with a fury that turned my knuckles white. "Then tell me who betrayed us. Give me that truth, Dominic, and I swear there will never be another door between us again."

The moment the door flew open, he was there. No hesitation. No anger. Just arms, warm, trembling, pulling me close, anchoring me against the chaos. His face burrowed into the curve of my neck, and I realized I was clutching him, not to push him away, but because I needed something —I needed him—to stop me from breaking into a million pieces.

He said nothing, just held me, breathing me in like I was oxygen and he'd been drowning.

My chest ached and my hands tightened on his arms as if I could hold the world together that way. My lower lip quivered, my eyes stung so I blinked as fast as I could to stop the moisture gathering there.

"I'm sorry, my love," he murmured, voice low and rough as shattered stone. "I failed you. I failed her. But we will find her."

His nose grazed the column of my neck, stopping beneath my ear. "Just... don't shut me out. Don't leave me outside while you bleed alone."

He shuddered, breathing in my presence like it was the only thing keeping him from falling apart.

"I couldn't bear it, Brooklyn."

"She's gone, Dominic." All the fight left me and I sagged in his arms. "I turned the city inside out and I can't find her."

"We will look together again." Tightening his hold, my mate shifted slightly and picked me up. "Two sets of eyes are better than one."

"You don't think I can be objective?" Scoffing at the insult, I debated jumping away from him, but it felt so good to feel the warmth of his body that I decided against it. He started walking down the hall, but I couldn't care less where he was taking me as long as I could steal the heat from him. I didn't realize how cold I was until that very moment.

"You?" He glanced down at me with a slight curl on one side of his lips that looked so sad I felt a pang under my ribs. "Objective when it comes to those you care about?" His hair had grown longer than he usually wore it, so it tumbled around his face when he shook his head. "Never.

Objective is not a word I would associate with you in this situation, my love."

"You're an ass." I thumped his chest with the back of my hand, and we both stiffened.

"You sound like Alice," Dominic muttered as he resumed walking after faltering for a second.

A lump formed in my throat the size of a fist, and I had to swallow it before I could speak. "Where are you taking me?" Ignoring the comment was in our best interest at that moment.

"I need you to see something." The offhanded way he said it shot adrenalin through my veins and I braced in his arms as if he would deliver a physical blow.

"See something?" My voice broke from the strong thrumming of my heart in my throat.

"See someone, I should say."

There was not enough time to interrogate him further before he took the stairs two at a time and rushed us downstairs toward the kitchen.

I hoped with everything in me that I could kill whoever it was. There was a mountain of wrath inside me and it needed an outlet.

I prayed Dominic would deliver it.

Chapter Two

ALICE

I couldn't remember the last time I drank this much; Hell, not even when I was bleeding out and Samir fed me his own blood to keep me alive after we'd clawed victory from the jaws of death with Brooklyn. Back then, I was half-dead, barely hanging on, but even that hadn't left me feeling as wretched as this. I did feel horrible for making my friend drown in guilt for accidentally hurting me but that was a different kind of torture.

Maybe we celebrated too hard, too fast. Maybe I got drunk on the relief of her recovery and the joy of still being here, both of us whole in ways that once seemed impossible. Maybe I lost track of the liquor the same way I lost track of time at the moment. Each blink felt like it lasted a second and an eternity. I mean, can you really blame me for losing track? Brooklyn was herself again, and that kind of miracle deserved to be drowned in every bottle within reach.

I would take victory wherever I could.

Those Syndicate bastards could go suck on a cactus for

all I cared. We won. Again. Us, two. The Council, zero. Victory tasted sweet… but its hangover hit like a vengeance.

My groan vibrated inside my chest, sending another wave of nausea through me. I probably shouldn't have downed the booze like it was my last day on Earth, I thought to myself. The laugh that rose inside me died the second bile curled up my throat like a cruel reminder of my predicament. Acid churned in my gut, turning my limbs into cold stone, though I was aching to jump up and pester Brooklyn with the flood of questions I knew she hated.

Not because she truly hated me. No, she acted tough because deep down, she was terrified. Scared to let herself feel, to be exposed. Because love, be it romantic or platonic, leaves a mark. And when it's taken away, it shreds you raw. I understood that fear more than she knew, but I refused to let her bury herself beneath it. I'd drag her humanity out into the light even if it tore me apart. Hell, it nearly did.

But it was worth every inch of pain to see her and Dominic finally let the walls crumble. Watching them open up to each other was like watching the sky tear open at dawn after endless night. I was a sucker for happy endings, always had been, and the sight of them accepting their feelings for each other made me want to cackle like some unhinged witch from a forgotten fairy tale. I'd do that later though. Right now, my head was ringing like some cursed cathedral bell and the floor threatened to slide out from under me every time I cracked an eyelid open.

Darkness swelled around me, thick and velvety, and far too alive for my piece of mind. It wrapped around me like a shroud, with streaks of color flashing through it, chaotic, hallucinatory brushstrokes slashing through an otherwise lifeless canvas. Some flared for a heartbeat at the edge of my vision, others twisted and writhed, slow and sickly, crawling across my sight like blooming nightmares.

Was I buried alive? The thought crept in cold and sharp out of nowhere, tightening my chest.

I squeezed my eyes shut against the hallucinations, willing them away, praying for a breeze, a whisper of air, anything to prove I was still part of the living world. Maybe Rowen slipped some herb or something in my drink as a payback for messing with him? I wouldn't let it pass him. He's been finding his sass in the time he spent cooped up with us in that house. My thoughts were as erratic as my heartbeat as they jumped in nonsensical manner from one thing to another.

And then it came. The grinding shriek of metal on stone that froze my entire being. So distant it echoed like a memory, something important that I should remember, yet sharp enough to cut through my fog and dissipate the urgency faster than the quick flashes of light. The sound clawed its way into my ears, absurdly loud and yet far away, turning my brain into mush.

Instead of freaking out, I found myself thinking, what kind of rusted gate had we installed in Samir's pristine damn house? He'd murder us if we scratched his beloved polished floors. The absurdity of the thought made a smile tighten my cheeks and pull at my lips. Small, shaky. But real.

Somewhere in the madness, my humor was still alive. And that meant I was too.

"Grab hold of her other arm." A hushed voice spoke urgently, sending alarm-bells pinging through my foggy brain.

Rough fingers wrapped around my limbs and that was enough to shoot adrenalin through me, strong enough to make me jerk and flop in their hold like a fish out of water.

It was a couple of people fumbling around, trying to grab hold of me while I flailed wildly, in erratic jerks, trying my best to dislodge them from me.

"I told you…Oomph!" One of them sounded pained when he grunted the moment my knee connected with the soft tissue of his abdomen. "Get hold of her arm before she wakes up fully."

"What do you think I'm trying to do?" The anger from the other person slithered like a snake over my skin when he hissed close to my ear.

My limbs were still heavy but fear gave me strength I shouldn't have had. I redoubled my efforts to prevent them from taking firm hold of me while trying to remember how I found myself in this predicament. In increments, details returned. The attack at the house where Guardians came in droves across the large expense of the yard and on the roof of Samir's safe house. Red bursts of magic spraying from my hands, killing everything in sight. Bodies turning into husks as soon as I grabbed hold of them while Brooklyn and Dominic fought with everything they had to keep anyone from hurting me.

That made me pause.

Without thinking too much about it, I stopped flailing and the moment I felt gold clammy hands latch onto my forearms I crossed my arms and grabbed onto the attackers the same way they clutched me. I had no idea what I expected to happen as I held my breath and all of us stopped scrambling for purchase as if they didn't know what possessed me that I'm holding onto them like my life depended on it.

I cracked an eyelid open.

The faces looming over me wavered from the stabbing

pain in my retinas but the shocked widening of their eyes was comical nonetheless. All three of us froze, holding our breath in anticipation but nothing happened. My attackers didn't shrivel into husks, no red magic shot through my fingertips to punish them for assaulting me. There was nothing apart from the staccato thrum in my ears from my heartbeat.

"Shit," I slurred as they looked at each other, their gaunt faces coming clearer into view. All anticipation and fear disappeared, leaving only determination hardening their features. "Shit, shit, shit."

"Grab her." The one on the left lurched forward and twisted my arm back so he could yank me to my feet. "She has no magic."

I dwelled on that comment as I hung awkwardly in his grip, twisting sideways until his buddy grabbed my other arm. In seconds, they had me suspended between them, my hair falling like a curtain over my face, hiding them from sight. I remembered making a dome around Brooklyn and Dominic to protect them from the never-ending swarm of Guardians, feeling my life drain into it with every hit it took from our attackers. Then… nothing.

Someone must've snatched me and dragged me.

My feet scraped over rough terrain as the two of them hauled me along, my body hanging limp between them. The stench of unwashed bodies clung to the air, making my nose wrinkle—and that's when I noticed my glasses were gone. Maybe that's why everything around me looked so blurry and misshapen.

"Remind me again why this is a good idea?" the other person, who was silent until now spoke, the words mumbled under his breath like I was too heavy to carry. The nerve of these guys. It wasn't like I asked them to drag me around like a ragdoll. My huff of annoyance was lost under the heavy sigh from the first guy.

"She asked us to bring her the new prisoner." The reverence in the tone was unmistakable. Whoever *she* was, this guy made it sound like she was a goddess he worshipped. "We are alive thanks to her. The least we could do is bring her the girl when she asked."

"We won't be alive for long if those monsters return and find her missing." The other one grumbled. "I thought the whole point was to stay invisible so we could keep our head on our shoulders. This is not staying invisible at all."

"They never return fast. It always takes a couple of days, you know that."

"Yeah well it only takes one time for them to return the next day for us to pay for it."

"Just shut up and move faster."

My mind was reeling while they bickered. No matter how much I wanted to pretend otherwise, it was clear that I'd been captured. With everything in me, I hoped my friends were alive because I knew without a shadow of doubt that Brooklyn would never let anyone take me if she could help it. Dominic wouldn't either, and as much as I gave Samir a hard time, grandpa would tear them apart to protect me as well. So, they were either incapacitated or dead if I was here. Fear like I'd never known embedded itself into the marrow of my bones.

No.

I refused to even think that. I needed to get my head clear, figure out where I was and get the hell out of Dodge. Then, I'd find my friends and hear the story about what happened from them. Yeah, that sounded like a perfect plan to me.

"I can walk." My voice sounded raspy and raw.

"What?" They both stopped, painfully jerking my arms in the process. The bossy one took hold of a fistful of my hair and lifted my head to look at me. "What did you say?"

"Did I stutter?" My annoyance turned into a hysterical giggle because I sounded so much like Brooklyn at that moment. I only wished I had her strength as well. I would've dismantled their limbs for drugging me and losing my glasses.

"Whatever they gave her muddled her brain," the second guy grumbled again as if this whole thing was too much of a hustle for him. Me too, buddy, me too, I wanted to say but couldn't summon enough strength to argue with him.

"I said." With everything in me I placed one foot flat on the ground, then after a couple of failed attempts, placed the other firmly enough to be able to straighten and wiggle my arms out of their hold. "I can walk. No need to drag me around."

To prove a point, I stuck my nose in the air and took one step forward. As life would have it, I didn't lift my foot high enough and my toes stabbed the hard ground with a sharp pain. My whole body lurched forward, and I only had enough time to throw both hands in front of me to soften the fall. All the air whooshed out of me when I face planted between the two men.

"Did she knock herself out?" The one who had been complaining the whole time sounded as if my clumsiness was a personal insult to him.

"For your information," I said, affronted, forcing the words past my slightly swollen lip—the result of my teeth meeting the inside of my mouth when I introduced my face to the ground. "I can't see well without my glasses or I never would've tripped." It was a lie, but they didn't need to know that.

"I don't have time for this. They can come back at any moment and find her gone. There will be no hiding this time." The bossy one snapped and grabbed my hair to pull me to my feet.

The gasp of pain that escaped me was cut short by a low, predatory rumble from the darkness—a growl so menacing every hair on my body snapped to attention. Fear prickled across my skin, and my breath froze in my chest. Slowly, I lifted my head, pushing the hair out of my face, only to find myself dangerously close—face to face—with one of the largest creatures I'd ever seen.

My insides shriveled as my eyes locked with its bright green stare. The rest of the world blurred without my glasses, which, in a twisted way, dulled some of the terror clawing at me. If I were about to get eaten, I'd rather not see it coming.

My mouth opened—maybe to plead, maybe to scream —but before a sound escaped, a blast of strange energy slammed into all of us, scattering bodies like bowling pins. Voices rang out, distorted and distant, as if underwater. I recognized the two men shouting above me, but their words were lost beneath the agony ripping through me—my skin peeling from my bones.

Darkness came out of nowhere and like a wave picking up sand on the shore it took me with it. Grateful to let the pain fade, I willingly followed.

Chapter Three

BROOKLYN

"None of this was my idea." Chester stood up and backed off from the table with both hands up in the air like that would've saved the demon if I wanted to end his life. "I swear it," he added earnestly, his Adam's apple bobbing as he swallowed thickly.

"I swear I don't understand how someone hasn't killed you by now." Echo groaned where she sat next to him, covering her face with both hands, her braided hair falling over her shoulder with the movement. "You are an embarrassment to all demonkind."

"Some of us have pretty strong self-preservation skills, I'll have you know." The demon rubbed his bald head while throwing nervous glances in my direction where I lay cradled against Dominic's chest. "I'll take your mockery over her fangs in my throat any day of the week."

I had a lot to say to those two, but my words turned to ash in my mouth when my gaze landed on the third person in the room—sitting at the head of the table, shoulders hunched like his body was trying to fold in on itself. Samir lifted his head very slowly, the motion laborious and seemingly painful. When his sunken, red-rimmed eyes locked on mine all the anger drained from me immediately.

"She's still alive." Samir words came slow and deliberate, his eyes fixed on mine—as if it were just the two of us in the room. "I can feel she is still alive but cannot track her."

Taken aback by how much Alice meant to Samir, I wiggled in Dominic's hold so he would put me down. "You and Dominic trusted the witch." I didn't mean to sound so accusatory, but I didn't regret my words. Not even when Dominic flinched under their weight. "I should've known he would betray us."

"He didn't betray us," my mate muttered, reluctantly releasing his hold on me, although he shifted his stance so the back of his hand brushed mine as we stood shoulder to shoulder. "They took him along with Alice. I truly believe that." His unblinking gaze conveyed the conviction he clung to, and when I glanced sideways at him, I saw the truth he believed written all over his face.

My eyes drifted back to Samir. He sat frozen, staring at his clasped hands, as though the answers were etched into his skin, visible only to him. I expected rage, accusations, threats about what we'd do when we got our hands-on Rowan. Anything would've settled my nerves better than the hollow, disconnected way he sat there, eyes fixed and unmoving. Watching him, a nagging feeling inside me told me he knew more than he was letting on.

Unwanted memories coiled through my mind, dragging me backward—to another time, another version of this room. We were sitting around this same table. Rowen cooking, Alice buzzing with excitement over her experiments with demon magic.

"We should hit at the cages. I doubt that they had enough time to fix all the damage we did when you got me out. I kept them busy enough with my bloodlust to make sure that they don't have the time to rebuild it. That's where we should hit. That's their weak spot," I remembered saying.

"I agree with you." Samir stood up and leaned on the table to bring himself closer to my face and look me in the eyes. "I don't know what we are going to find there, Brooklyn. And I shall hope you will not hold it against me, whatever it is. I made a promise that you would live. I never made a promise to be a good and kind male. To keep our word, one must do atrocious things sometimes. I am not proud of it. Any of it. I do not regret it, however. And let us not forget. I am an Atua. I do what my nature demands."

"Yeah, okay, we get it. You're an asshole. We knew this so there's no need for additional demonstrations." Alice grabbed his shoulder and shoved him away from me with surprising ease. "Can you get out of her face now? Dear God, are you all this theatrical, all the time? Everything must have drama and suspense with you guys. We agree we need to attack tonight. Let's get dressed, and let's go. We can discuss Samir's shortcomings when we come back and there is cheesecake."

Was there more to Samir's words that night that I didn't examine closely? Was he trying to warn me of what was to come and I dumbly ignored it, chalking it down to Samir being his usual self? Was it truth instead of arrogance coming from the ancient Atua? Nausea made the room spin for the longest moment, and I had to breathe deeply through my nose so I didn't drop like a rock.

That uneasy feeling redoubled its efforts, bringing bile to burn the back of my throat.

"Do you agree with Dominic, Samir?" My attention stayed locked on him, even when I moved to the far end of the table where Echo pulled out a chair for me. The female was too aware of me at all times—which would've put me on alert at any other time. I was grateful for it at the moment though. Because the longer I thought about that day when we planned the attack, the weaker my knees became, and I had to sit down before I crumbled at Dominic's feet. "Thank you." I squeezed Echo's hand in gratitude, noticing how warm her skin was compared to the clammy feeling of my palms.

She noticed too because she threw me a worried glance that no one but me noticed.

"Don't mention it," she murmured but continued to peek at me worriedly.

"I do not know what the witch did or did not do." His tone came off too defensive to remove my doubts or apprehension. "All I know is we need to find the human before it's too late."

Frantically searching for Alice and drowning in guilt for not preventing the Council from taking her didn't leave me much space to think about who was to blame. Rowen took Alice and carried her to Frederick which automatically placed him as the number one suspect and the person I needed to blame and kill. But was he to blame or was he just making sure one of us stayed with Alice to help her until the rest arrived for a rescue? From the corner of my eye, I watch Echo narrow her gaze on Samir as well. She'd picked up on the defensive tone too, it seemed.

My heart jumped in my throat when a wet nose bumped the back of my hand where I was clutching my knee under the table. It was turning into a habit to physically hold myself together. I pushed the chair back slightly so I could lean to the side to see the wolf staring at me with a million questions in his too wide eyes. The damn thing should've shifted by now, knowing Alice was in danger, and not for the first time I thought this may not be the person I thought he was. Was it a simple wolf I mistook for a shifter? The desperation and the intelligence staring back at me from under the table said I was not wrong. It was the damn shifter my friend decided to keep as a pet. And there he was, still a wolf.

"Great help you are." I took him by the snout and shoved him away from me. "What good are you to Alice if you can't help her when she needs you?"

"He's been searching every night just like the rest of us." Dominic jumped to his defense. "We had to patch him up a few times. Not sure if it was Atua or just street dogs he fought."

The wolf just stared at me, despair clouding his too-round irises.

"This is what I wanted you to see." My mate grabbed the wolf by the scruff and pulled him out from under the table. "Two days ago, we tended to this wound, but instead of healing, it's getting worse. I thought it might give us an idea on where to look next for Alice."

Upper lip curled in a snarl, the wolf glared at Dominic but didn't try to bite him. He allowed himself to be pulled like a stuffed toy so the bandage I hadn't noticed until then could be removed. I had to physically fight my reaction to the pungent stench coming from the ugly looking cut at the animal's side the second the gauze was pulled away.

"Nasty," Chester chirped from over my shoulder, leaning in to see what we were doing—only to let out a grunt of pain when Echo elbowed him out of the way. "What? It's not like they don't know it's rancid. Their sniffers work better than mine," he grumbled.

I couldn't disagree with the demon. My eyes watered from the funky, acrid odor smacking me in the face. Dominic pushed the fur as far as he could without hurting the wolf too much yet it must've been too painful anyway. The creature whimper-growled, aware we were trying to help him but still hurting enough to not be able to stay quiet.

"That looks familiar." My eyes locked on Dominic's. I could see him remembering the wound I sustained from the poisoned dagger when they rescued me from the cages. The same poisoned dagger which turned me feral and crazed with bloodlust.

"You two want to share?" Echo was stretched over the table to see the wolf at my feet. "I haven't evolved enough yet to read minds and everyone in this house is too good at having mind conversations the rest of us are not privy to." She cocked her eyebrow at me. "I can't help if I don't know details."

She had a valid point, so on an exhale, I scrubbed a hand over my face and waved at the seeping wound with the other. "He was cut with a dagger coated in poisoned blood." Ghost pain throbbed on my own body with the memory. "The same poisoned blood that pushed me into bloodlust not long ago." I saw Dominic's fist tighten in the fur he was holding.

Echo's eyes widened and Chester whistled from behind me. "The wolf found them then?" The male demon started pacing, his footfalls even and purposeful. The tempo of his strides strangely calmed my racing heart.

"I don't know if he found them," my mate snapped, yanking on the fur in anger. "I told him to take me wherever he was injured like this and he won't move a paw outside the damn house."

As subtly as I could, I lifted my gaze to check on Samir who'd been suspiciously silent through all this. The old Atua looked too pale as he stared at the wolf, his gaunt eyes too big for his face. His words came slithering through my brain like vipers. *I made a promise that you would live. I never made a promise to be a good and kind male. To keep our word, one must do atrocious things sometimes. I am not proud of it.*

A wet nose bumped the back of my hand where I still clutched my knee in a white-knuckled grip. My eyes darted to the animal, snapping me out of my thoughts.

"You found where they are squatting," I told him. Not a question but a statement. He watched me steadily. "You know I will do anything to get Alice back safely, don't you?" That earned me one slow, tentative blink. "Will you take me there?"

For the longest time the wolf searched my face, debating whether he should trust me or not. I would've thought he knew by now how much Alice meant to me, but if he was the shifter I was sent to kill, I couldn't blame him for having his doubts. I didn't trust my own kind further than I could throw them either. My gaze jumped to Samir again, just a quick glance to see him staring at us with a very peculiar expression on his face.

My chest tightened.

The wolf whimpered, snapping my focus away from the ancient Atua and pulling my full attention back to him.

Slowly, very slowly, he lowered his snout in a barely-there nod.

"You will lead me to them?" I asked again to make sure we understood each other. Adrenalin shot through me, warming my insides instantly.

Another nod, faster this time.

I rose from the chair, rolling my shoulders to release the tension bunching my muscles there. "I guess we have places to be, people to see." Dominic was already on his feet, checking his weapons before I finished the sentence. You can join us if you like," I said to the room in general.

"I thought you would never ask." Chester clapped his hands gleefully, an evil grin spreading across his face.

Samir stared at me mutely, not standing from the chair.

I needed to find Alice. I'd deal with everything else later. Turning my back at him, I strode to the door, yanking it open with an ominous crack. I heard a chair scrape the floor behind me, but I didn't turn. I took Dominic's hand when he offered it and didn't check to see if Samir followed.

I could always kill him after I had Alice safely home.

Chapter Four

DOMINIC

I used to believe I'd already met Hell on Earth.

I thought I knew what it meant for your soul to ache, truly ache, when my entire family was ripped away from me in the most gruesome ways imaginable. For so long, I was numb. Revenge became my lifeline. That was an acceptable existence. Clean. Simple. Until my mate barreled into it and shattered every wall I'd built, forcing me to feel everything I never wanted to feel.

And then, the Fates reminded me: you can still wither inside. You can claw at the ether, gasping for breath, even after you thought you'd drowned.

They gave me Brooklyn. And then they poisoned her blood. They dangled her life in front of me, a carrot on a string, reminding me just how easily they could rip her away, too. I remembered the old philosophy: if you are afraid of dying, you will not live.

But that wasn't it.

I wasn't afraid of dying. Never that.

I was scared shitless—for her.

Watching Brooklyn fall apart as Alice was taken... It stripped me raw from the inside out. Her guilt chewed through her like acid, and I could do nothing but watch. Powerless.

Helplessness was a curse I wouldn't wish on my worst enemy.

I was worried for the human, yes, but not like Brooklyn was.

They had something, the two females. A bond I couldn't name, couldn't wrap my head around. I had horribly miscalculated how deep that connection ran. I almost lost Brooklyn when Alice was gravely injured. She unraveled before my eyes, piece by fragile piece.

And just when I let myself breathe, just when Alice began to heal, the cursed Council took the human.

And here I was again: blind with fear for Brooklyn, sick to my stomach thinking of what they were doing to Alice.

"I don't think it's a good idea to split up," Echo murmured, barely audible, like that would somehow stop us from hearing her.

"I don't need an escort, Echo." Brooklyn's voice was so tired that it cleaved through me like a blade. "I won't do anything impulsive to jeopardize Alice's life."

A week ago, I would've called that madness. Brooklyn, not acting on impulse.

But now? Now I believed her.

There was something behind her eyes, quiet and sharp and terrifying. It should have scared me. Hell, it should have scared all of us.

But I trusted it to protect her. Trusted her to take calculated risks.

Brooklyn's fury was a wildfire; Consuming, blood-chilling...but this?

This was something else.

Something colder.

Something that didn't burn...

It froze.

My thoughts churned, and I nearly flinched as a shiver crept down my spine. We'd already reached the garage, rows of Samir's vehicles resting in stillness beneath their pristine covers. The air inside pressed in, heavy and expectant.

The silence noticed me. And I, foolishly, noticed it back.

The air thickened more, breathless, until ghostly fingers traced the nape of my neck. My body tensed, instinct coiling tight, every nerve whispering run.

I turned, slowly, unwilling to shatter the moment and found her eyes waiting.

Brooklyn watched me, her focus so absolute it stripped everything away. It was just the two of us.

Her gaze pinned me in place, sharp and intimate, and for the first time in a long while, something primal within me stirred—fear, ancient and bone-deep, whispering that I wouldn't survive this.

She arched a brow, her lips curling into a half-smile that had broken lesser men.

"What?" she asked, velvet over steel. "Nothing to say to that?"

I blinked, once, twice, trying to shake the weight of her presence. But she carried gravity now—pulling, inevitable and relentless—I was helpless to resist.

Brooklyn had always been beautiful, dangerously so. The kind of beautiful that drew glances, then stares, then hearts. But this was something more. A shimmering, electric hum beneath her skin. An enchantment I could feel in my teeth.

And it wasn't just me.

The male demon, eyes wide and vacant, began to sway toward her, hypnotized. He moved as if lulled by music only he could hear, a snake lured by the piper's spell. Echo looked dazed as well. The wolf whined miserably, curling in on himself, tail tucked under his trembling body.

And in that moment, I understood.

Whatever this was, whatever she was becoming, it was no longer just mine.

It was still my mate, I could feel her heartbeat in my chest, just as mine echoed in hers.

But there was something more now.

Something darker.

Something ancient.

And, strangely, I accepted it… even as it terrified me.

"You don't need to explain yourself," I said, though my voice trembled more than I liked. The moment the quiver broke free, her smile deepened, and I hated that she noticed.

My animal paced restlessly in the background, unsure if he should take over or disappear entirely.

"I'll follow you anywhere, mate," I said. "All you have to do is lead the way."

A long moment passed.

Whatever was hiding behind Brooklyn's gaze stepped forward, measuring me, stripping me bare.

I prayed fiercely, silently, that it would find me worthy. Because there was no doubt in my mind—I would fight the gods themselves to stay by my mate's side, and I would die trying if I had to.

One breath dragged through my lungs, thick and heavy, every inhale a struggle against the weight of the air.

Then, suddenly…

A pressure burst.

The weight vanished.

It was as if the world sighed and let me breathe again.

"You truly mean that," Brooklyn murmured, soft as starlight, and completely unconcerned that we weren't alone.

"I will defy Death to stay by your side, Brooklyn." With an iron will, I forced my body forward and took her fingers gently into mine. "The Fates can't be that cruel to finally give you to me, only to take you away."

Her chilled skin warmed beneath my touch.

I clung to her fingers with the desperation of a drowning man grasping dry straw. She stepped closer, our bodies brushing. I could feel the soft curves of her pressing into me, and it hit me just how long it had been since I'd truly felt my mate.

"You speak the truth," she said on a breath, lips barely parting.

"With everything I am."

Echo cleared her throat, shattering the moment, but Brooklyn didn't let go.

In fact, her fingers threaded deeper between mine, tightening the hold. A silent promise. An understanding. I hoped she felt it too.

"I'd hate to be..." Echo began, only to yelp and leap backward with a startled shriek.

"If you hated it, you would've kept your trap shut," Chester growled, glaring as he held up a clenched fist, strands of her hair dangling like a prize. "That was the most beautiful moment I've ever witnessed. And you ruined it."

"You truly are preposterous!" Echo gasped, rubbing the spot on her head where the strands had come loose. "Did you seriously just pull my hair?"

"I thought tearing off a limb might be too dramatic." He sniffed, shrugging. "Don't make me regret it." He ducked just in time as her fist swung for his head.

"We should go," Brooklyn said with a quiet chuckle, shaking her head. "Before the children burn down the garage."

All I could do was stare at her, struck dumb. I hadn't heard her laugh in what felt like forever.

Another link in the chain around my chest loosened.

"What?" she asked, ducking her head with an awkward smile, tucking a stray strand of hair behind her ear.

"Don't shut me out. Please." I pressed my forehead to hers, cupping her face as I breathed her in. "I'll do anything you ask. Go anywhere you lead. Just... don't push me away. I want to help bring her back."

"I know." She surprised me with a soft kiss, barely a brush, but it lit fire along my lips.

"Let's take the fastest car," she added with a wicked grin, "just to annoy Samir a fraction of how much he annoys me."

"How about this one?" Chester called out, bouncing beside a dust-covered Bentley.

Brooklyn's eyes gleamed with a wicked glint. "I'll drive."

"Whoop!" Chester pumped his fist victoriously, still clutching Echo's hair like a trophy.

"Yeah... I think I'll drive." I darted toward the car, tugging my snickering mate behind me.

"She doesn't know how to drive, so do not encourage her," I growled at Chester, who wisely kept his mouth shut.

"Get in." Brooklyn opened the rear door and ushered the wolf inside before sliding in after him.

Echo joined them, leaving Chester and me to take the front.

I looked across the hood at the demon. "I hope I can count on you to watch my mate's back."

Chester's usual humor faded. "Our interests align, shifter. As long as they do, I'll protect her with everything I've got. If they don't…"

He left it there, but the message was clear. His loyalty had an expiration date.

I respected his honesty. I gave him a firm nod.

The car purred to life as I gunned it out of the garage.

In the rearview mirror, Brooklyn's eyes met mine. She knew me too well. My subtle nod was returned with silent understanding. She'd heard everything. And she believed him too.

I just hoped I wouldn't have to kill the demon any time soon.

He was starting to grow on me.

Chapter Five

ALICE

It was always cold here.

Not the kind of cold that made you shiver and rub your arms, but the kind that sank deeper—into your bones, into your thoughts. The kind that whispered you were alone, even with someone standing right in front of you.

I didn't know how long I'd been here. Time didn't move properly in this place. The light—or whatever passed for it —the constant, sickly flicker of muted green, never shifted. The walls stayed damp. The silence pressed in, patient and listening.

And I hated it.

Curled up as tight as I could fold my body, I hugged my knees to my chest fiercely to prevent the violent shaking racking my frame.

I think I was imagining things as well. Monsters lurking in dark tunnels. Men dragging me half conscious, bickering amongst each other that they had to take me somewhere before someone else came. Someone else meaning the Council.

The two remaining asshats that were left, that was.

A crazed snicker escaped me, and I had to press my trembling hands to my mouth to stifle it.

They thought they could break me.

And maybe, on some days, they got close.

Those days when I woke up screaming, soaked in a fear that didn't belong to me. When the chains around my wrists burned even though they were cold. When I swore I heard Brooklyn's voice in the dark, only to realize it was my own mind playing tricks on me. Yes, on those days, I thought maybe they'd done it, cracked something in me.

But I wasn't shattered. Not yet.

Not while I still had my friend, my sister.

I didn't know what they did to me, not exactly. I only knew that things weren't right. That the air buzzed too loud when they entered the room. That sometimes, I felt like I was glowing beneath my skin, lit up like a candle from the inside, and it hurt. Dear Universe, it hurts. But worse than the pain was not knowing if my friends were safe.

Brooklyn and Dominic mostly. I couldn't imagine a world without them, although I had to admit I cared a bit too much for the others, as well. The demons included, even though I barely knew them. Having their magic pass through me made me understand them better on some molecular level. Like I wasn't weird enough before all this shit.

Not for the first time, I wondered if there was some merit to my father's crazy ramblings about aliens and conspiracies. What if supernatural creatures did things to him that he couldn't explain so he created this world of extraterrestrial beings following him around? His poor mind could've been messed with because of me.

Because of whatever I was.

Isn't it a damn fate years later after his death to meet the most wonderful people, a new chance at having a family and a friend everyone wishes for but rarely gets, only for bastards to want to use and control us. To destroy us on a soul level.

If they'd hurt my family to make me do whatever they wanted, I would never forgive myself.

Especially Brooklyn.

She had been the anchor in my storm, the one person who didn't flinch when the darkness crept in behind my eyes or when I did the most ridiculous and insane things. When I was slowly changing and turning into who knows what. Brooklyn stood firm. She saw something in me. Something I wasn't even sure existed.

Now I held onto that thought like it was life itself.

Like it was blood.

Because if she was still out there, then I had to survive until she found me.

And she will find me, I said firmly to myself.

I would survive.

Even if I had to pretend to be broken.

Even if I had to smile at my captors like I didn't dream of ripping their spines out.

Even if I had to become something they didn't expect.

They thought they had me.

But I've played the game of pretend before.

And this time, I wasn't playing to protect myself and blend in.

No.

I was playing for Brooklyn. For Dominic.

And all the gods and the universe help anyone who tried to stop me.

I didn't hear any footsteps or anyone nearing the dark,

damp room where I was kept. The walls here had a way of swallowing sound, like everything sacred had been devoured long ago.

But I felt it.

That shift in the air.

A ripple of something slick and venomous sliding into the room.

I didn't move. Didn't even lift my head. I stayed curled against the wall like I hadn't noticed.

"Alice," came the voice, silken, amused, and serpentine. "That is your name, is it not?" when I didn't answer or acknowledge his presence he continued. "Still playing martyr for those who abandoned you without a second glance?"

I almost laughed. Still playing, he said. Like my pain was an act. Like my strength was theater. I can feel the fucker Frederic leering at me from a few feet away. The last rat clinging to the throne of a sinking ship.

He moved closer, each step deliberate, calculated. The scent of cinnamon and blood enveloped him, a sickly sweetness masking decay. His power pressed down on me, an unseen hand gripping my throat, squeezing my lungs.

"Must be exhausting," Frederic whispered, his voice threaded with mock sympathy, "pretending defiance will save anyone." He crouched beside me, long blonde hair falling over his shoulder and hiding half of his face. "We both know how this ends, don't we?"

I didn't answer. I focused on keeping my breathing shaky, my eyes dull, like I was barely there. Let him think I was broken. Maybe he will go away.

He sighed theatrically. "I have an offer." His voice lowered conspiratorially. "You help us…genuinely help us…

and you'll see your little band of misfits again. Safe. Unharmed."

Slowly, deliberately, I lifted my gaze to meet his. "And in return?" My voice was fragile, vulnerable, just as he wanted. My friend would be proud if she saw my acting skills.

The idiot crouched next to me bought my act.

Frederic smiled sharply, the beauty of his features distorted by cruelty. "You let us harness what's inside you. Accept your true potential and do our bidding. Imagine the power you'd hold. You'd be revered, feared, unstoppable." He leaned in closer, his words baiting me like poison-coated apple. "Brooklyn would live, Dominic too. All you have to do is surrender yourself fully to us. Become something greater."

A beat of silence passed. I let my eyes shimmer with just enough unshed tears. Let him think he'd won something. I could feel him gloating and the excitement bubbling, buzzing under his skin.

Then I smiled. Small. Hollow.

"I'm already something greater," I whispered.

His expression flickered.

I leaned forward, slow, every part of me humming like a drawn bowstring. "And if you so much as touch one hair on Brooklyn's head again," I said, voice sharpening like frost across steel, "you won't live long enough to beg for death."

Frederic's eyes widened, but only for a second. Then he laughed. Light, mocking. But he stepped back. Just one step. But I saw it.

He was afraid.

From me.

The absurdity of it almost made me scream-laugh in his face.

"Such spirit," he said, standing straight again. "You'll

learn soon enough the only room for you in our world is on your knees. You'll learn your place. We all do."

He turned to leave, but paused at the door.

"Oh," he added without looking at me, "when you start glowing again, try not to scream too loud. We have new guests in the lower levels who are dying to meet you. Don't want to disturb their rest."

And then he was gone.

The door shut softly behind him, plunging the room back into its oppressive quiet.

He thought he knew me. Thought he could control me. But he didn't see the truth.

I would figure out what terrified him about me, then I would use it. I had every intention of escaping before Brooklyn risked her life to save mine.

They thought they almost broke me, but I was just getting started.

Chapter Six

BROOKLYN

Something was wrong.

Not the low, constant hum of anxiety I'd learned to live with since Alice was taken.

No. This was different.

Sharper.

Colder.

It came out of nowhere, sharp enough to steal the air from my lungs. Something reached inside me, clamping down on the place where my instincts lived, bruising it from the inside out. Pressure built behind my ribs, twisting along that invisible cord tethering me to her—the bond I hadn't asked for, hadn't wanted at first, but couldn't live without now.

It was the only thing assuring me my friend was still breathing.

I stared out the window as we drove, trying to focus on the blur of motion, absently listening to Dominic mutter vocal responses to the wolf for our benefit. They communicated on some animalistic level none of us was privy to.

Buildings passed. Places I might've cared about once. None of it mattered. None of it had color. Not while she was still somewhere under the Syndicate's thumb. Not while she was hurting.

"She's not okay," I breathed, more to the glass than the people around me. "Something's happening to her."

Dominic's eyes flicked up in the rearview mirror, meeting mine. He didn't ask who. Of course, he didn't. He knew. They all knew.

Echo shifted beside me in the back seat, her boot tapping anxiously against the floorboard. "That means she's alive," she said quietly. "You'd know if she wasn't." I could see it in her eyes that she spoke from experience, probably when I killed her brother.

I ignored the tightening in my chest.

"That's not the point." My voice came out sharper than intended. I forced a breath through clenched teeth. "I can feel her… like she's wrapped in chains that keep tightening. She's not screaming for help. I don't get that feeling. That's what scares me."

Dominic's hands flexed on the steering wheel, the leather creaking beneath his grip.

"She's gone quiet," I whispered, rubbing at the center of my chest desperate, to return whatever link had formed between us. "And when Alice goes quiet like that… it means she's close to the edge."

Not the kind of edge you fall off. The kind you jump from, full of fire and fury.

The kind of edge you don't come back from unchanged.

"She will do something dumb, she won't wait." My eyes locked on Dominic's in the rearview mirror. He understood better than anyone how reckless our friend was when she thought she was protecting us. "She'll get herself killed."

I'd seen it before. Those moments when the world pushed her too far, when everything cracked and she stopped trusting people to save her while the rest of us were in danger. Alice didn't break like others. She shattered inward, then reformed herself into something harder. Colder. Sharper.

And she never warned you before she exploded in a flurry of random magic.

"She's waiting for something," I added, voice low. "Planning."

"Good," Echo muttered. "Let her plan. Let her burn them from the inside while we strike them from the outside. I'm sure we are nearly there."

I didn't answer. Because I didn't want that.

I wanted her alive. Whole. Safe. Still Alice.

Not the version of her the Council was no doubt trying to make. Not the ghost they'd hoped to carve out of my best friend. The same ghost they carved out of me for decades.

I leaned back and closed my eyes briefly, trying to reach her again. Not with magic. Not with any power I could name. Just with... us. With the thread we'd tied between each other somewhere between disaster and laughter, blood and kindness.

The bond shimmered faintly, tension rippling through it with every subtle shift.

I didn't hear her voice. Not exactly. But I felt her: bruised but upright. Hurt, but furious. A wildfire behind cracked glass.

She wasn't asking for help.

She was waiting.

And that was worse.

"She's going to do something," I said aloud, my eyelids snapping open. "Soon."

"She's always doing something," Dominic muttered.

"This time feels different." My throat ached. The wolf whimpered from between Chester's knees where he was fidgeting. "This time I think she's preparing to become something the rest of us won't recognize in hopes of helping us."

A heavy silence settled in the car. Even Chester had gone quiet in the front seat, for once not running his mouth. That alone made my skin crawl. He kept digging the nail from his forefinger into the skin of his thumb, his eyes vacantly staring at the window. His profile was carved out of stone.

"She's not just surviving," I whispered, a lump growing in my throat. "She's preparing for war."

I swallowed thickly, forcing the panic down.

No tears. No spiraling.

Not now. Not yet.

Because Alice didn't need my grief. She needed my rage. She needed me focused. Ready to kill for her if it came to that. And I was. Dear gods, I was.

She'd always been my roots, pulling me back to the earth when I wanted to drift off and follow the breeze. Always patient, always understanding, even when I was a walking nightmare of trauma and venom. She stayed. She saw me. Not the chaos. Not the blood.

Me.

And now she was in their hands.

And I was supposed to stay calm.

The guilt and fear tried to swallow me whole again, drown me in the misery of my thoughts but I fought it with everything in me. If I succumb to it, the Council will win.

Let them keep her long enough to make their last mistake. Let them think they'd broken something precious.

I would burn their empire down brick by brick just to put her back together.

"Brooklyn," Dominic said, softly, "We're close."

I nodded once.

"Then we go in, fast. Quiet. Anyone in our way..." I paused, tasting the venom on my own tongue. "...dies screaming."

Echo smiled. "Now that's the Brooklyn I know."

I turned toward the windshield, the road stretching into darkness.

The Council thought they knew who they'd taken.

They thought I would break.

They didn't realize they'd just unleashed the weapon they created.

And when I finally got to Alice...

I wasn't just bringing her home.

I was leaving Hell behind me.

The road narrowed into gravel, then dirt. Trees closed in on either side of us, their branches, gnarled and skeletal, scraping at the sky. Dominic turned off the lights and slowed down. The deeper we went, the quieter it became. No birdsong, no wind, no life. Just the rumble of tires over stones and the soft, ominous whimper of the wolf.

There were predators lurking near; nothing dared breathe.

Then, like a wound splitting open in the earth, the forest gave way.

We pulled to a stop at the edge of a clearing, half-shrouded in mist and shadow. And there it stood.

A mansion.

The mansion stood like a bastardized echo of my old life; A distorted version of the place I'd once called home.

The cages beneath it still counted, I supposed.

It hadn't rotted. It hadn't collapsed.

It waited, just like they did.

It was massive, three stories of cracked stone and ivy-choked windows. Most of the roof had collapsed inward, and sections of the façade looked scorched, like someone had tried to burn the place out of existence and failed. The gates had long since rusted off their hinges. Nature had tried to reclaim it, but the mansion refused to rot. It sat like a corpse that hadn't learned it was dead.

"Looks abandoned," Echo muttered, leaning between the front seats squinting through the fog.

"It's not," I replied without hesitation. I could feel the monsters in wait behind those walls.

She didn't argue.

Dominic cut the engine and eased the car behind a line of trees, parking under the cover of overgrowth. We got out slowly, every movement deliberate, ears straining. The silence wasn't natural. It was held. Like the land itself was holding its breath.

"No wards on the perimeter," Chester noted, running a hand along the air near the trees. "Not the usual kind, anyway."

"They don't need them," I said. "They want us to think there's nothing there. They are hoping no one would be stupid enough to look twice."

I stepped forward, gaze locked on the windows.

"I don't like this," Dominic muttered, his animal prowling restlessly behind his green gaze. "We are too exposed. They didn't pick this place for nothing. It's strategic."

"Which means it's a trap," Echo finished for him, inching closer to Chester, the two demons testing the area for witch magic and wards.

"Of course, it's a trap." I crouched and swept a line through the dirt with my fingers, eyes narrowing. There were fresh tire marks leading around the parameter instead of straight to the front steps. Barely visible, but there. "They've been using the back road."

Chester tilted his head. "Think she's in there?" Red circles of demon magic spiraled around each of his arms.

"I know she is." The words came out ice cold. "She's in there; I can bet my life on it. And they know we're coming." Rolling my shoulders didn't help remove the crawling feeling under my skin.

"We could wait till dark," Dominic suggested, squinting at the darkening sky which still had shades of light gray and blue in it. "Send the wolf around the perimeter. Check for Guardians. Get the layout. I'll shift and go with him."

I nodded. "Do it."

The wolf bolted off into the brush without hesitation, paws silent on the damp earth the second a black panther stretched his powerful body in the spot where Dominic stood not a second ago. I watched them go, jaw tight.

Echo stepped up beside me, scanning the structure. "We need at least two entry points. One silent. One violent. Some of us can keep them busy while someone takes Alice out."

"I'll take violent," Chester chimed in from behind her, cracking his knuckles.

"Of course, you will," I muttered, a smile tugging at my lips despite the rage and fear twisting in my chest. Chester was too calm, too cheerful to be real. There was rage churning behind those sparkling-with-amusement eyes of his ticking like a bomb.

I took a long, slow breath, trying to ignore the way my

pulse thudded in my ears. My eyes drifted back to the mansion.

Somewhere behind one of those blackened windows, Alice was waiting.

Maybe she didn't even know we were here yet.

If she couldn't feel the connection like I did, maybe she thought she had to do this alone.

She didn't.

I turned to the others, voice low and sure. "We go in tonight. Silent as we can. Split at the south wing. Echo and Chester cause a distraction. Dominic and I go through the cellar. No one lives unless they have to. Except Frederic."

Chester raised an eyebrow. "And if we have no other option but to kill him?"

"You'll have plenty of options," I said, voice flat as a blade.

Killing Frederic would be a mercy.

None of them deserved that.

We waited in the trees, every second stretching like a blade across my nerves. Dominic and the wolf returned just before the night spread over us like a blanket, furs matted with dew and eyes alert. The wolf gave a low huff and flicked his ears toward the west wing.

"There's a breach," Dominic translated the moment he returned to his human form. "Collapsed wall behind the overgrowth. Leads to a lower level."

Perfect. A little too perfect but so be it.

"They'll expect magic," I said. "They'll expect brute force. They'll expect me to blast the doors screaming. But they won't expect us to slide in through their broken history. No one would guess I'll go to the cages willingly."

"Just like old times," Dominic muttered, dozens of unsaid things swirling behind his eyes.

"No," I said, focus still fixed on the mansion. "Not like any other time." Slowly I turned to look at him. "This time… we finish it. Once and for all."

"What about the witch?" Chester sounded uncomfortable just mentioning the traitor. "Should we bring him back with us or…?"

Kill him—that's what he meant but didn't dare say. Chester was a wise male always picking his words so he doesn't step on any toes.

"Don't kill him." Dominic answered so fast the words were almost blurred. I cocked an eyebrow at that. "I want to know why, if he was the one who betrayed us."

I stared at him.

"You can kill him after I have a talk with him." My mate offered an olive branch. "If he did it."

"With pleasure," I said truthfully. "And I can't see how it was not him."

Chester shivered, a full-body shake rippling through him. "Brrrr. I'd hate to be on the receiving end of that."

"I'd keep my mouth shut then." Echo shoved him as she moved past. "Let's go kill some Atua before she decides to kill you first."

Chapter Seven

DOMINIC

The night didn't breathe.

It crouched over the clearing like a beast waiting to pounce, heavy and still. Fog clung to the base of the trees, curling around our legs. The mansion loomed ahead, ruined, rotted, waiting.

We moved fast. Silent. Focused.

Brooklyn stalked through the overgrowth like she was born to it, hand signals quick and precise, eyes sharp and determent. She was a storm bottled into flesh, and if Alice wasn't in that place, I knew she'd bring the whole damn building down just to make a point.

I'd help her do it.

I kept my steps light. The wolf mirrored me on the opposite flank, ears twitching with every distant creak or shift of wind. With a whispered good luck, Echo and Chester peeled off to the east to cause their very special brand of chaos.

Brooklyn and I headed west toward the breach the wolf and I had found: a collapsed portion of the mansion's wall, now hidden behind thick ivy and decaying stone. It led to the lowest level, likely some old servant's entrance or storage chamber. Somewhere no one watched anymore.

Except someone was watching.

I cursed myself for not paying closer attention before.

The scent hit me first. Sharp and oily. Burned ozone.

Witch magic.

I froze mid-step, holding one arm out to stop Brooklyn behind me. The wolf beside me snarled, hackles rising.

Too late.

The trees exploded around us.

Shadows peeled themselves off trunks and the ground, condensing into shapes with glowing eyes and rotted mouths. Blackened armor cracked and groaned as if it hadn't been moved in centuries.

"Witches," I hissed, already moving. "They're summoning ghouls."

The ghouls came fast. Unnatural. Silent. Weapons like bone scythes and shadow-tipped spears raised high. Their first target—my mate.

My heart shriveled in my chest as the first weapon was aimed at her.

I should've known better.

Brooklyn ducked the first strike with fluid grace, sliding beneath a curved blade and driving her elbow into one ghoul's side. He didn't grunt. Didn't react. Just reeled back and swung again with robotic violence.

I didn't wait anymore.

My bones snapped and reformed mid-step. Pain lanced through me from shifting twice in such a short time, but I welcomed it. It was real, grounding. My body stretched, fur tore through skin, and my animal took shape around my thoughts.

I dropped to all fours in a rush of heat and teeth.

The world sharpened.

Smells became knives. Sounds exploded like firecrackers. Every flicker of movement came with intention.

But my mind was still mine.

Alice. Protect Brooklyn. Kill anything that stands in the way.

I lunged at the nearest ghoul, jaws wide. My fangs sank deep into its thigh as it swung toward Brooklyn. The crunch of bone filled my ears, but it didn't scream. Just tried to pivot toward me with mechanical precision.

Blindly, I ripped at it, tearing it limb from limb.

It fell.

More came.

Brooklyn moved beside me like fury personified, kicking, slashing, calling on something old and mean that lived in her bones. We fought back-to-back, the way we always did when things got ugly.

A ghoul got too close. I spun and slammed into its side with my shoulder, throwing the weight of my feline body into it. We crashed into a tree. I felt ribs crack, his, not mine.

They were stalling.

The realization hit me like a brick. They weren't trying to kill us.

They were trying to keep us occupied.

Which meant…

"They know we're here!" Brooklyn panted, hurling a ghoul into a patch of dead ivy. "They're buying time for someone to move Alice or until the Council gets to us!"

I roared, tail lashing, claws finding the next threat. "We go now! No more waiting!" I thought to my mate.

"Echo and Chester…" She shook her head as if reprimanding herself. "They'll catch up or they won't."

I growled my agreement, swiping through another ghoul's chest. It fell in pieces while two others took its place.

Brooklyn didn't wait for more encouragement. We broke toward the breach in the mansion, the wolf taking the rear.

Two Guardians blocked the path the moment we pushed through the brush, standing shoulder to shoulder like two boulders preventing our way in. I didn't slow. I launched. Before my mate could reach them, my body collided with them both, claws slashing, teeth tearing, and for one heartbeat, it felt like they had no weight at all. Just air and ash wrapped in skin too thin for my claws.

Brooklyn slipped past me, darting into the opening, vanishing into shadow.

I followed, heart pounding, blood roaring in my ears.

Inside, the mansion breathed. Not with air, but with memories. Pain clung to the stone like mold. Chains and old screams lingered in the cracks. Familiar scents assaulted my nose so hard I was dizzy enough that my sight blurred.

I shifted back mid-stride, panting hard, chest rising with every breath.

"We're in," I said, voice hoarse. "She's close. I can feel it."

But Brooklyn didn't look back. Her shoulders were squared, her steps silent.

"We must find her, Dominic, or we die trying."

The air inside the mansion was thick, like stepping into wet ash. The temperature dropped by degrees with every step we took, but it wasn't just the cold that raised the hair on the back of my neck.

It was the feeling of being constantly watched.

Every cracked stone, every twisted beam above us remembered the evil that spread like a parasite through time. I could smell it in the walls, blood old enough to have soaked into the foundation. This wasn't just a prison. It was a shrine to suffering.

Brooklyn moved ahead of me in absolute silence. She didn't speak. She didn't have to. Her rage hovered just beneath the surface of her skin like heat waves, warping the space around her. She moved like she belonged here. Not as a prisoner this time, but as a reckoning.

I kept close behind, scenting the air, every muscle coiled. Magic brushed against my senses, faint, complex, and full of poison.

A sharp crack split the air ahead of us.

Brooklyn jerked back and stopped.

So did I.

A shadow moved at the end of the hall. Then another. Cloaks dragging across stone, pale fingers lit with runes. My vision sharpened to the curve of a lip twisted in amusement under the hood made of moth-eaten fabric.

Four witches emerged from the gloom like ghosts coming home. All female. All deadly.

"So disappointing. You're not supposed to be here," one of them said, voice silken and cruel coming from everywhere at once. "We had such high expectations of you, Brooklyn."

She didn't blink. "Yeah? Well, I'm fresh out of fucks to give, as Alice would say."

I barked out a laugh, unable to stop myself.

The witches moved as one, forming a half-circle to block the corridor.

My instincts screamed. These weren't novices. Their magic ran deep into the old blood, the kind that didn't need spells. It lived in the marrow. It was part of this place long before the building rose above it.

"We don't want to kill you, you have another purpose. Our fates depend on you and the prophecy," another said. This one was older, eyes too calm for my liking. "But we will because we have no choice, our hands are tied. The girl is not yours to take."

Brooklyn cocked her head. "She was never yours to keep to begin with."

No more words.

One of them struck without warning, a bolt of emerald lightning lancing through the air toward us. Brooklyn threw up a shield instinctively—her mother's magic coming to the front to protect her, the spell cracking against it like a gunshot. Her feet ground to the grimy floor, sliding back from the pressure. The impact pushed her back into me and I caught her, grounding us both.

Then we moved.

I shifted mid-leap, my body stretching into the sleek, familiar weight of my animal who burst forward willingly, eager to fight along our mate. No hesitation. No doubt. I hit the stone floor running, claws throwing sparks as I launched at the nearest witch.

She disappeared in a puff of smoke and reappeared behind me, but I was already turning, tail whipping to catch her in the ribs. She screamed, skidding across the floor, crashing into a crumbled archway.

Brooklyn was already in the middle of the other three.

She fought like the goddess of wrath had taken human form: fast, sharp, and unrelenting. Fire crackled from her hands, her boots moved like she knew the floor was about to betray her. Light, barely touching the ground. She wasn't holding anything back.

But neither were they.

One witch snarled and sent a wave of wind so strong it cracked the wall beside us. Brooklyn ducked, rolled, and hurled a spear of flame from her palm, striking her square in the shoulder.

That one didn't get back up. Smoke curled up from the heap under the cloak.

I tangled with another, jaws snapping inches from her throat as she tried to chant. She screamed when I sank my teeth into her arm. Magic fizzled and spat as her focus broke. Her blood hit my tongue, thick, bitter, burning.

I didn't let go until I was sure she wouldn't be casting again. My jaw released her only after she lost consciousness.

Two down.

The remaining pair circled Brooklyn now, weaving energy between them in a helix of blinding silver and black. They were chanting in a language long forgotten by men, faster now, braiding a shared spell that vibrated in the floor beneath us.

I shifted back just in time to warn my mate. "Break the link!"

Brooklyn didn't hesitate. She dashed forward, throwing a blade, not a spell, a blade, straight into the throat of one of them.

The spell shattered like a burst bubble. The second witch howled as her partner dropped, blood spraying across her robes. She barely had time to react before Brooklyn closed the distance and slammed her into the wall, ripping her throat with her fangs.

The fight was over in seconds.

My mate turned slowly to check if I was okay, bright red blood dribbling down her chin.

I'd never seen anything more beautiful in my life.

I caught her in my arms as she walked into me reverently like the blessing that she was, my breath still sawing in and out, heart still hammering in my ribs, body humming with magic and adrenaline.

Then I heard the scrape of a shoe over hard floor.

Footsteps behind us moving fast, uneven, unbothered.

Echo appeared first, eyes gleaming with residual magic. Her hands were stained with blood and something that looked like black sand. "Miss us?" Then she saw the witches around us. "Pfft. You two always end up having all the fun."

Chester was right behind her, brushing soot off his jacket. "We brought fireworks."

I rolled my eyes. "We're past the party, unfortunately."

Brooklyn didn't even look at them. She moved to check over the fallen witches, shoulders tight, breathing shallow.

"They're dead." Nudging one with the toes of her boot, she wrinkled her nose in disgust but her eyes were unfocused. "Alice is close," she said, almost too softly.

I believed her.

"Let's go get her," I said. "We'll think differently when she is with us."

Chapter Eight

ALICE

My misery redoubled, every bone in my body aching as I blinked myself out of the nightmare's hold. For a few seconds, I didn't know what woke me.

Then I felt it.

It started with the shaking of the floor.

Just a little. Like someone had dropped something very heavy one level above me. Then again, louder. A boom that rattled the ceiling, dust drifting into my hair like a warning whisper, and the chain on my wrist twitching like it wanted out as badly as I did.

Then came the shrieks.

The screaming.

Not mine, for once. Definitely not mine.

I sat bolt upright on the cracked stone slab they so generously called a cot, heart thundering like it was sprinting for the exit without the rest of me. The chain clinked in protest, a macabre rhythm of pooling rusted metal at my feet.

That wasn't the usual "ritual murder" ambiance the Council liked to provide.

What I was hearing was a fight.

Real combat.

Familiar chaos.

My mouth fell open before I could allow myself to hope. "No. Freaking. Way."

Another boom echoed through the floor. Dust rained down in a puff, and one of the glowing wards in the far corner of the cell flickered. My chain shifted slightly looser.

Holy hell.

Brooklyn was here.

I could feel her. I didn't know how, I didn't know why but there was no mistaking the surge of heat along my spine, the sudden punch of comfort and sheer defiance.

She was pissed.

And she wasn't alone.

"You beautiful, terrifying bitch," I whispered, a cackle catching in my throat. My hand pressed to the center of my chest where the bond pulsed like a war drum. "I was hoping you wouldn't but you actually came."

And then I stood up so fast I immediately headbutted the low stone beam above the cot.

"OW...damn it!" I hissed, stumbling back and clutching my forehead. "Okay. Still a prisoner. Still stupid architecture."

I blinked back stars and took in the cell again, really looked at it this time. The room was barely six steps wide. The walls were damp, streaked with mildew, the stones weeping condensation that stank of rot and despair. Old symbols glowed faintly in the corners, wards meant to suppress, to break down the will. It was like being locked inside a dying memory. Maybe that's why I felt so depressed all the time. No windows either. No sounds except for distant dripping water, groaning stone, and now the thunder of war.

I paced the length of my cage, every nerve on fire.

She was here. They were here. And I wasn't about to just sit here waiting to be scooped up like a lost puppy.

Nope.

I was meeting them halfway.

Even if I had to chew through the damn chains.

The shackle flared again, sparks licking across my skin, and I flinched. The ward in the corner pulsed harder now from dim to bright, like a heartbeat. Like it knew what was coming.

I narrowed my eyes at it.

"Okay, magic rock light… you and me are gonna have a moment."

It was now or never.

I'd been watching the witches, memorizing their movements, how their fingers danced when they cast spells, how they channeled energy through runes, how their faces went really pinched when they had to focus. I didn't have spells, not really. But if I could just fake it like I had faked everything else that worked so far…

I drew a shaky breath and held my palm up to the ward, closing my eyes. A picture of Yoda came to mind when he used the force in the movie, and I burst out laughing with no control. Okay, I was in shock and my brain was trying not to short-circuit by using humor. Collecting myself was harder than I would've thought, but I wrangled my crazy down. My hand lifted toward the ward again.

Immediately, the image of Yoda popped into my brain again, and I snorted.

Because obviously, my mind would reach for Star Wars in a high-stakes magical jailbreak.

"Focus, dumbass," I whispered to myself. "Loop. Flick. Spiral. Angry flick. You can totally do this because you are a badass bitch as well. Let's get cracking."

I mimicked the pattern I'd seen the youngest witch use, repeating silently in my head: loop, flick, spiral, angry flick. Then I added a dramatic chant for effect.

"By the crusty socks of chaos and the great hormonal rage of a PMSing woman during full moon, I banish you!"

…Nothing.

"Worth a try," I muttered, scratching at my forehead. I was running out of ideas.

The chain sparked again, this time harder. My arms trembled with something, not pain, but potential, maybe? My skin lit up from the inside like it had before, that horrible glowing sensation returning all over my body.

Except now, it didn't hurt.

Now, it felt right.

Mine.

I turned back to the glowing ward and with a running start slammed my palm flat against it.

"Let. Me. Out!" I shouted at it with everything in me.

The ward cracked loud enough to scare the hell out of me.

My eyes widened. "Well, hell." Urgency made me reckless. I had to get out of here to help them a little.

I did it again. "LET ME OUT!" I screamed at the ward, my voice lost in all the noise coming from above me.

A bolt of light surged through the chain. It shattered with a shriek of metal and a burst of magic that tossed me straight on my ass. I slid across the room like a ragdoll and hit the back wall hard enough to see every childhood trauma flash before my eyes.

"Motherfucker! Why is it always the landing that sucks?!" Grunting, I rubbed the back of my skull while staring at the ceiling.

I was free.

Holy shit I was actually FREE!

I scrambled up, heart pounding like I'd just been reborn and screamed into the world with a middle finger raised. I flipped off everything around me with gusto. I grabbed a broken piece of stone and a rusted rod from the corner, my makeshift weaponry, because sure, why not channel some feral raccoon chic energy today.

I'd rescued a few of those back in the day and let me tell you, those mofos are vicious.

I cracked the door open slowly peeking gingerly at the hallway.

Empty.

Of course, it was.

I crept into the corridor, tension coiled in every step. It was worse out here, darker. Like the walls absorbed all sound and hope. Every stone whispered a different scream. The air tasted like rust and bad dreams.

And beneath it all… the fight raged.

Closer now. Boots. Growls. Magic splitting the air like thunderclaps.

Something hissed from around the corner, the sound prickling my skin.

I spun just in time to see a vampire—okay I should call it an Atua since Brooklyn was very peculiar about it. But the fucker was pale, fast, and very not on our side since he was lunging at me. My hands flew up instinctively, one to hold him back and the other to protect my neck. I had no intention of being anyone's' juice box, thank you very much.

A pulse of energy shot from my palm and yeeted him into the opposite wall.

There was a meaty crunch and a small moment of silence where I stared at my glowing fingers and whispered, "Holy shit. I am the wand." A manic cackle burst from my lips.

The creepy guy was a pile of very dead meat on the floor, and I wanted to be anywhere but near him when they found him.

Cackling like a madwoman, I bolted down the hallway. Barefoot. Bleeding. Wild-eyed. I flung stolen magic like a toddler with paint. Improvised like my life depended on it, which, fair point, it did. At one point I shouted something in Latin-sounding gibberish and blasted a chandelier off the ceiling. Not helpful. It looked cool, though. No one cared if I was screaming or laughing. They couldn't hear me from all the kickass happening not far from me.

Then I turned a corner and hit a wall of pure magic like a goddamn freight train.

I crashed backwards into a pile of urns used as decoration in the damn place. One broke over my head. Again.

"Okay. So... maybe magic requires aim. And finesse. And fewer concussions."

But I was close.

I knew I was.

I could feel them, Brooklyn and Dominic, like bright stars in the storm guiding my way. Strong. Moving fast. Coming for me.

If I was discovered, I just had to hold on a little until my friends arrived.

I could do that.

I wasn't alone.

Not anymore.

That gave me a burst of energy I didn't know I had.

Gripping the iron rod, I pushed to my feet, determined, bloody, dizzy and laughing through my teeth.

"All right, assholes," I growled at the empty hallway in front of me, lurching toward the next corridor. "Let's play."

Chapter Nine

BROOKLYN

This cursed place was getting to me.

The deeper we pushed, the more it felt like the walls were closing in on me. Hissed voices reached my ears like the stones themselves were holding secrets; Not the kind you whisper. The kind you bury. The corridors were crooked, warped from time and cruelty, and the stench of old blood clung to every inch of it. I'd passed the same path once or twice but I'd never been this aware of everything. Never paid it this close attention. I wished I didn't at that moment either. Wished I could ignore the cracks splitting the floor like veins, and the strange sigils that had been scorched into the walls. Every so often, we passed alcoves with charred bones still chained to the stone, forgotten offerings in a house of horrors.

I didn't need a reminder that this place was soaked in death. My skin knew it.

My own blood was soaked in the very core of the cursed structure.

So was my rage. And I clung to that with everything in me.

Dominic and I moved in silence, his hand occasionally brushing at the small of my back like he was reassuring himself I was still with him instead of buried in memories. Usually that would've made me upset, but I appreciated it this time—more than he knew. The wolf was slinking through the corridors nose brushing the ground, searching for Alice as hard as we were. Echo and Chester were just behind us, close enough that I could feel their magic humming through the stale air even when I couldn't see them. We'd just finished dragging the bodies of the last witches we encountered, and my body ached from the strain, but I didn't stop. Couldn't stop.

Alice must be close.

Closer than she'd been since the Council took her anyway.

Just as I thought that, a sharp agony doubled me over, nearly dropping me on my knees. It took me a second to realize that it was not me that felt pain but Alice.

Something was wrong.

Again.

I paused at a junction, hand pressed to the grimy stone to hold myself upright, breath shallow, sweat slicking my temple despite the cold. The air here had teeth, biting at my skin, every nerve bristling with warning.

Two halls diverged before me, dark and gaping, the space heavy with the threat of something ancient stirring just beneath the surface.

One curved upward toward a splintered staircase barely clinging to the wall, its steps broken and warped by time and disuse. Faint whispers of light filtered through the cracks above, chasing shadows like they were afraid to linger.

The other sloped down. Into blackness. Not the passive kind, but a darkness that felt alive. Sentient. Hungry. It reached for me without moving, promising the kind of pain you don't come back from the same.

I didn't flinch.

I didn't need to.

Because the pull in my chest, that invisible thread tied to Alice, snapped taut, strained to the edge of breaking, the weight of it crushing every breath.

There was zero doubt in my mind.

She was down there.

And she was running out of time.

My heart tripped.

"She's below us," I whispered through numb lips, well aware of what was down there.

Dominic stepped beside me. "You sure?"

"Yes."

Not a question. Not a hunch. A certainty that rang through my bones. The bond pulsed again, almost violently this time. Alice wasn't just below, I could tell that she was moving. Alive. Desperate.

"She must've escaped wherever they held her," I said, dread spreading through my limbs just thinking what she could find there. "She's trying to meet us, the crazy female."

"That explains the tremors," Chester muttered from right behind me. "Your girl has quite the chaotic signature when she starts flinging magic like she was born with it."

"She does, doesn't she," I snorted, ignoring the comment about her acting like she was born with it. He was more observant than I gave him credit for and I'd hate if I had to kill him now. One, the demon started growing on me. Two, Alice was a priority.

"We should double back," I said, straightening and forcing the tremor from my voice. "There's a split by the antechamber. If we take the lower hall there, it loops around the core foundations. We'll find the entrance to the cages level."

"Brilliant," Chester muttered. "Just what I wanted, spending time around cages."

I turned a sharp look on him, but he only shrugged, unapologetic. His meaning rang clear—*I'm just saying what everyone's thinking. They're the ones too scared to say it.*

"What else will we find?" Echo asked, her voice low, blade already in hand. She ignored her companion so naturally I had to bet that Chester had a habit of being a smart mouth when the stakes got high. I had no time to make a comment about any of it.

Never got a chance.

As if summoned by her question, the wall beside us let out a deep, splintering groan. The stones shuddered beneath our feet, dust sprinkling in fine streams from the ceiling. We all took steps back, plastering closer to the walls in case the roof caved in on us. A cold draft curled through the corridor, creeping along the back of my neck, too slow, too deliberate to be just air passing through. It carried the scent of damp earth, rot, and something older. Something feral.

The scent of ozone burned my nostrils.

A sound followed.

Low.

Rhythmic.

Wrong.

It was chanting.

At first, it was just a whisper beneath the groaning stone, like wind curling through freshly sprouted leaves. But then it grew. It layered. Many voices humming in perfect, hypnotic unison. No melody. Just purpose. As if the building itself was being called to attention.

I felt the magic behind it before I saw anything. A slow tightening in the air, like pressure building beneath my skin. It scraped across my bones, foreign and invasive.

Dominic stiffened beside me, his nostrils flaring, his animal instincts rising fast. He grabbed me around the waist and tucked me behind him in a too smooth of a motion.

"They're calling something," he said, voice roughening.

"Or someone," Echo added, already backing into position next to him. The red sigils etched on her blade began to glow.

I unsheathed my dagger sliding sideways so I could flank my mate on the other side. I'd be dead before I'd hide behind him when there was danger. He rumbled unhappily but said nothing.

Smart male.

The stone beneath our boots throbbed faintly now, as though the structure was some enchanted beast that was awakening, its heartbeat restarting sluggishly at first but getting stronger with each thump.

"They're trying to make sure we don't reach Alice," I said with the certainty etched into my bones. The magic felt wrong, but I understood it deep down, my blood was answering its call without my permission. "Or, if we reach her to not be able to leave. It's a magical trap."

"Get ready." Dominic growled. He was already shifting, bones cracking and reshaping into something leaner, sharper. The panther dropped beside me with a thud, his tail lashing, eyes glowing faintly in the dim light.

"Back to back," I pulled on Echo's arm to get her moving closer. "We keep each other's backs. Don't let them isolate you. I'll do my best to hold a shield against their magic for as long as I can. You three kill anything that moves within reach."

They came from the shadows.

Five this time, maybe more behind them. Robes like smoke. Eyes gleaming with silver flame, sigils pulsing eerily on their skin. They didn't hesitate. One threw a bolt of pure force at us. I raised my hand instead of forming a shield, catching it mid-air and absorbing the energy into my palm with a snarl. For a split second I felt the shock on the faces of those around me but I had no time to think what that meant. Taking a page from Alice's book, I decided to own it, as she would say.

"Wrong move," I hissed at the equally shocked witches, and hurled the cursed magic back.

It struck one in the chest and slammed her into the far wall with enough force to crack the stone, impaling her like a bug. Dominic launched forward, claws flashing in the gloom, and tore through the wards shielding another. Chester and Echo moved as one, coordinated in ways I never thought they could be, slicing and searing with brutal elegance. It was a deadly dance that flowed as if we'd practiced it for years.

A witch tried to flank me, her blade drawn with poison dripping from its edge. I ducked under it and drove a pulse of energy into her chest. She screamed as her body crumpled into the far pillar. Another tried to bind me in glowing sigils, but Echo's blade severed the witch's arm before the spell finished. Chester hurled his dagger across the room. It sang through the air before burying itself in the last witch's throat.

I fought with the strange power rising in me, as if it had always belonged there.

The magic came easier now. Wilder. I didn't question it.

A scream pierced the air. Not one of ours. The final witch collapsed, her mouth open in a silent curse.

We didn't stop to check if there were more waiting around the corner.

We ran.

Down, around, through the suffocating dark. The walls were narrowing now, the ceilings were getting lower. Archaic carvings lined the stones, pulsing with low, green light. The air grew thicker, hotter, reeking of rot and old blood. Before I was ready to accept that I was back where everything started, my boot scraped over flat dusty packed ground.

We reached the lower hall.

That's when the Guardians came.

I barely had time to shout a warning before they were on us.

Guardians.

More grotesque than before, skin stretched taut over bulging muscle, their armor fused to flesh like it had grown there. Leather harnesses held jagged swords and hook-blades, their faces hollowed out into masks of decay. And those eyes...dead, sunken things, pierced sharper than any weapon. They saw nothing, felt nothing. Just vessels of pain and purpose.

Dominic met them head-on, all fang and fury, a black blur of muscle and teeth. I followed, slicing through one with a blast of pure kinetic force still humming at my fingertips. It shattered the Guardian's weapon, sending bone and steel flying as his body slammed into another.

Chester was laughing, actually chortling, as he hurled a Guardian up the staircase like a ragdoll. Echo was right behind him, a goddess of flame, igniting another with a flick of her wrist. Their demon magic danced between them in spiraling arcs of fire and shadow, scorching symbols into the walls.

The wolf, blood-soaked and feral, darted between the bodies, jaws clamped around a thigh. He ripped. Twisted. Shook it like a toy. Viscera rained across the stone.

Screams rang out, echoing off the ancient stone. Sparks skittered across the floor. Steel rang like a choir of bells as it kissed stone and bone. I ducked a swing, rolled beneath a Guardian's reach, and came up in a slash that tore open a ribcage. Hot blood sprayed across my neck.

Dominic launched off the wall and crashed into two of them mid-air, dragging them down in a whirl of snapping teeth and howls. Chester barked a command, the runes around him erupting into light as the ceiling groaned and part of the tunnel collapsed, crushing a wave of rein-forcements.

I prayed Alice wasn't behind that wall of stone.

But I couldn't blame Chester.

I'd have done the same.

Echo and I moved like we shared a single spine. Her fire drove them back; I carved the opening. She scorched limbs; I severed spines. A macabre duet of survival.

We thinned their numbers, step by bloodstained step.

The bond in my chest screamed now, a tether yanking me forward with the urgency of a pulse about to flatline. She was near. Right there.

"Alice, stay back!" I roared, unsure whether I wanted to

warn her, or just hear my voice. Hear something other than the madness.

Another Guardian lunged, his jaw unhinged wide like a predator unmasked. I didn't hesitate. I drove my blade through his throat, twisting until vertebrae cracked like glass. His body fell like a puppet with its strings cut.

Then…

There.

At the far end of the corridor, past shattered pillars and half-burnt tapestries, stood Alice.

Her hair was a wild, tangled mess around her face in sweaty ringlets. Her skin was smeared in blood, some hers, some not. The rusted pipe in her hands was lifted like a sword, trembling slightly in her white-knuckled grip. Her mouth split into a grin so broad it nearly cracked her bruised cheeks.

"We killed the fuckers!" she shrieked, voice sharp with unspent adrenaline. The pipe wobbled above her like a flag of chaotic triumph.

She had no glasses. Of all things, my brain snagged on that like the absurdity of noticing an earring missing during a shipwreck.

But gods, she was alive.

I didn't wait. I ran to her, weaving between the wounded, dodging the fallen, blood splashing beneath my boots.

Nothing else mattered.

Except nothing in this damn life was ever that simple.

Just as I reached the final stretch between us, three more Guardians emerged from a hidden alcove to block my path. Bigger. Meaner. And they weren't alone.

From the shadows behind Alice came a voice. Cold. Familiar.

"I was wondering how long it would take you to find her," purred Frederic.

Of course.

Of course, he was here.

Unfortunately for him, I was done running.

Chapter Ten

ALICE

I should've known it was too easy for me to get to a point where I could see my friends. Stupidly, I didn't think anything of it until it was too late. Shuffling forward with strength I didn't have, I started to doubt that I was out of that damn prison. Maybe my nearly broken mind conjured a story where I was free and almost away from the hellhole they kept me in.

The corridor still echoed with the chaos of battle, shouts, metal ringing, the sharp coppery sting of blood in the air. My knuckles were raw, the rusted pipe shaking in my grip, and yet... when I saw Brooklyn charging toward me, I felt safe. I shouldn't have. Not here. Not ever around the bloody vampires.

But my friend was a blazing star in the dark, unstoppable, blood-slicked and radiant with fury. She was coming for me. Tearing everything and everyone apart that stood in her way.

My knees almost buckled from the relief.

That was when the shadows behind me twisted.

I barely had time to turn before a cold arm wrapped around my throat and dragged me back against a hard, immovable chest. A blade pressed under my chin, the prickly metal biting at the tender spot there. I froze, sucking in a sharp breath as fingers like ice clamped down over my shoulder.

"I was wondering how long it would take you to find her," purred Frederic, his voice curdling the blood in my veins.

Brooklyn's eyes snapped wide as her feet skidded to a stop a few yards away.

"What a lovely reunion." he cooed beside my ear, silken and sharp as a razor. "How very touching." Long strands of his silky blonde hair fell over my shoulder when he grazed the tip of his nose on the side of my face, sniffing me.

That sleazy asshole.

Of course, it was him.

I'd never seen Brooklyn look so murderous.

"Let her go, Frederic and I might kill you quickly," she growled, each word soaked in venom.

"Mm-mm." He tutted, dragging me back a step into the deeper gloom behind us. "Not unless you'd like to see what color your dear friend is on the inside."

The blade nicked my neck. I held still, swallowing hard. My hands gripped the pipe tighter, but one wrong twitch and I was dead. I knew that. So did he.

None of us moved.

Not Echo. Not Chester. Not Dominic, who'd shifted back to his human form and stood like a coiled spring, nostrils flaring. His eyes still glowed faintly with his animal close to the surface, darting between Brooklyn and me like he was debating which way to pounce if the opportunity presented itself. Even the wolf was frozen in place although it was obvious how badly he wanted to come to me. His body was trembling from the effort to stay put. I hoped he'd listen because I'd hate to watch him being killed.

"If any of you so much as breathe the wrong way," Frederic continued conversationally like we were all out for a stroll, "I'll slit her throat from ear to ear. And wouldn't that be tragic, Brooklyn? You fought so hard to save her... only to watch her die at your feet."

"I dare you, do it," she whispered, all emotion disappearing from her face. It was as if someone else who looked exactly like Brooklyn stood there, but it wasn't her. Her power flared so hot the very walls groaned with it. "See what happens to you, Frederic, when I have nothing holding me back."

Frederic only smiled wider.

"I believe I've said this before," he drawled, and I almost gagged when he shifted, bumping into me, and I felt his erection poke my lower back. The creep was getting hard from the prospect of killing me, or from taunting Brooklyn. Either way, it was disgusting. "But you're magnificent when you lock your humanity away. I cannot wait to have you back where you belong. Your friends started joining us already and they are waiting for you to come home."

So, it was from taunting Brooklyn. He was repulsive.

Then I felt the power creeping toward me and every other thought drifted away. A ripple of vile magic sliding through the air like oil. My stomach turned.

From the shadows behind Frederic, another figure emerged into the flickering torchlight.

"Rowan!" Brooklyn's voice hissed with so much venom that even I flinched.

My breath hitched like it had been knocked from my lungs.

It was Rowan.

Same bold head. Same long worn cloak. Same eyes, only... they weren't his bottle green peepers. They were dull. Vacant. Like a puppet waiting for a string to be pulled.

He didn't blink.

Didn't speak.

Didn't even see us.

"Oh no," I breathed. "Rowan? No, no, no."

"Look who joined us," Frederic said brightly while bile rose in my throat. "I left him alive. I simply found a better use for him." Sounding disappointed, he started shaking his head and the blade dug deeper into my skin. "He was a horrible witch anyway."

Brooklyn took a half step forward, eyes wide, shaking her head. "Rowan? Rowan answer me." My friend used that tone in her voice which forced anyone to obey her but not a muscle moved on Rowan's face.

"He can't hear you," Frederic interrupted. "He's quite... borrowed, shall we say? A rather exquisite blend of witchbinding and possession. Nasty business, really. Messes with the soul, I've heard. But, on the bright side, he's terribly obedient."

The old vampire removed his hand from my shoulder, and his fingers twitched once in a graceful motion at the dazed witch next to us.

Rowan moved.

Fast.

Straight toward Brooklyn.

A scream lodged itself behind my teeth, but I didn't dare move. Thankfully, she dodged just in time, sliding back as Rowan's hands lifted in front of him and lit up with intense visible energy, blue-white sigils sparking like lightning around his fingers. He threw a wave of that energy at her, and it cracked the stone floor where she'd been standing a second ago.

"No!" I screamed, struggling in Frederic's grip. Damn him and that knife he held on my throat. "Let me go, you piece of shit!" I slammed my elbow back into his ribs, felt the impact, but he didn't even flinch. I was about to slam the pipe I still clutched in my other hand but I immediately froze. Magic shivered down his arm and tightened like a vice around my neck and shoulders. I was paralyzed from neck to waist.

Brooklyn didn't strike back, I realized in horror.

She couldn't.

Her expression was carved from agony and restraint, but all she did was dodge every attack from Rowan.

"Fight back!" Chester roared, trying to rush forward, but Echo slammed a hand across his chest, preventing him from coming between Brooklyn and Frederic. Her eyes blazed.

"She can't fight, you idiot!" Echo hissed. "Not until Alice is clear!"

Brooklyn ducked another blast, then rolled, narrowly dodging a rune sigil meant to turn her insides into wall decorations.

Rowan advanced like a whirlwind built for destruction. Precision in every movement, methodical, calculated. He launched another spell, this one a narrow beam of scorching light that sliced clean through a support column beside Brooklyn's head.

She dropped into a crouch, rolling through a plume of shattered stone and heat, her body a blur. Sweat gleamed on her brow as she rose behind the debris, breath ragged, gaze finding mine for the briefest, electric second.

The anguish there nearly undid me.

She wanted to end this. She wanted to kill Frederic. She wanted to protect me, as she always had, more.

But she couldn't. Not without sentencing me to death.

And Frederic knew that all too well.

"Oh, the poetry of it all," he murmured, his voice a velvet blade curling against my ear. "Your lethal little guardian, reduced to inaction by sentiment. How tragic."

"You'll regret this," I said, jaw clenched so tightly my teeth ached, vision blurring under the weight of whatever power he used to squeeze my ribcage.

"Possibly," he replied with a languid shrug. "But regret is a game for mortals, darling. And I'm rather immortal, I'm afraid."

Rowan struck again, this time summoning a corkscrewing vortex of fire and electrical charge that shrieked through the air. Brooklyn dodged by inches, landing hard against a jagged outcrop of wall. Blood trickled from a gash along her temple, yet she pushed up again without hesitation, without fear.

She never paused.

Behind her, Chester strained against Echo's restraining hand, his expression a storm of wrath and desperation. The wolf prowled in tense arcs, jaws frothing, a low growl reverberating through the stone like a bad omen.

"Brooklyn," Dominic was as still as a statue as he growled, his voice roughened with urgency. "We need to go. We can return another day for Alice."

"No," she bit out, ducking as another arc of sigil-fire seared past her cheek, singeing the ends of her hair.

"Anytime you want to start fighting works for me, female!" Chester bellowed, eyes darting between Rowan and the blade still pressed to my throat. Something had freaked out the demon but I had no clue what.

Frederic's hand twitched, and agony bloomed through my ribcage as the invisible bindings forced me to my knees. The pipe clattered to the floor beside me like a useless relic from my paralyzed hand.

Brooklyn took a step forward, arms lifted; Not to attack, but in supplication. "Rowan," she said, her voice taut with urgency and sorrow. "Rowan, it's me. You don't have to do this. Please. I know you didn't betray us. Dominic assured me. Fight him." Her voice took that tone again. "Fight him, Rowan."

But Rowan didn't blink. His hands continued to dance, sigils flaring brighter, more intricate, twisting into incantations designed to dismantle souls, not just bodies.

"Brooklyn!" I choked, panic rising in my throat. "You have to stop him…he's going to kill you!"

Her eyes flicked to me, burning with quiet resolve. "I won't risk either of your lives."

"You'll risk your own?!" I cried, heart clawing against its cage.

Her answer was simple. Unflinching.

"Always."

And then the air shifted.

Not just temperature, but something deeper, like the architecture of reality had flinched. The sigils in Rowan's hands began to sputter. His arms shook.

Frederic's pleasant mask twisted in displeasure. "Oh, don't tell me the puppet has found a string of his own."

In a blur of motion, Brooklyn sprang, not toward Rowan, but toward me. Her blade arced like a falling star, a desperate gamble, a calculated risk.

Frederic snarled, yanking me backward, tightening the bonds he had around my upper body. Magic snapped around my limbs, pain coiling through my spine like barbed wire.

Brooklyn couldn't reach me in time if he decided to jerk the blade across my neck but it forced Frederic to shift his focus. Just long enough.

The spell holding me paralyzed weakened.

I moved.

I slammed my head backward, catching him between his legs right over his erection. There was a scream, a satisfying, shrill shriek, and his grip loosened.

I dropped to the floor and seized the pipe, still slick with my own blood and sweat.

And I swung with everything in me.

The blow struck his kneecap with a sickening crunch. He howled, magic flaring wild around him and then, without fanfare, he vanished. Dissolved. Like mist into the night.

He was gone.

The crushing weight on my chest evaporated. The bonds fell away.

I hit the floor, coughing, lungs burning, every nerve frayed to the quick.

"Rowan…" Brooklyn whispered inching slowly to place herself between me and the witch.

He stood as if suspended, mid-cast, arms trembling.

"I know you're in there," she said, softer now, each word a balm and a plea. "Don't let him do this to you. Don't let him erase you."

His lips parted. A faint breath escaped.

"I… can't…"

But he hesitated.

Brooklyn moved with excruciating care, inching forward, her palms still raised.

On the other side, Echo leaned toward Chester, voice barely a whisper. "If he lashes out again, I'll stop him. Possessed or not."

"No," Brooklyn said, keeping her eyes locked on Rowan's. "He's one of us. And we don't kill our own."

Rowan's fingers spasmed.

And then… his knees buckled.

He crumpled to the floor, unconscious, blood trickling from his nose and down his chin.

The sigils around him flickered out like extinguished candles. The tension dissolved, leaving only silence. Thick, aching silence.

I stood trembling, everything inside me clenched tight. The iron pipe was still clenched in my hand, streaked with sweat and blood. It felt like a joke now, absurd in its inadequacy after everything we'd just endured. But I held onto it anyway, white-knuckled and shaking.

My gaze met Brooklyn's.

Then the adrenaline gave out.

The room tilted sharply. My knees turned to water. I wobbled a step forward, but the floor was a wave and I was drowning on it. The stone walls swam in and out of focus, growing dimmer with every blink.

"Brook…" I started, but the word didn't finish. My voice failed me.

Everything became a blur.

I saw her move before the floor started spinning and I lost my footing. Before the darkness swallowed me, I felt my friend's arms catch me so I didn't hit the ground.

"I got you," she said, and I was lost to the dark.

Chapter Eleven

BROOKLYN

We had to move.

The moment Rowan collapsed and Alice slumped against my chest, everything crystallized with a cold clarity. The silence surrounding us wasn't safety, it was the breath drawn before the scream. Frederic wasn't dead, much as I longed for it to be true. He hadn't even been injured badly enough to grant me a fleeting illusion of justice.

No, he was regrouping. Somewhere in the bowels of this cursed stronghold, he was gathering his wretched forces again, sharpening the blade he meant to drive through us.

And he would return. To gloat, to punish, to claim what he believed was his.

I shifted my grip on Alice, securing her limp form against me as her head lolled gently onto my shoulder. Her pulse, though faint, beat steadily against my fingertips, a fragile rhythm that was enough. She lived. That was all I needed.

But she couldn't walk. And Rowan…

"Is he breathing?" I asked, my voice sharp with urgency.

"Yes," Echo answered grimly. "But just barely. He won't wake anytime soon."

Dominic didn't speak although I could feel his eyes on me, checking if I was injured without getting me upset by fretting over me. He merely lifted Rowan's inert body over his shoulder like a burden he had carried a thousand times before. The witch hung lifelessly, limbs dangling, his face pale and hollow, as though the spell that had bound him had scraped out his soul and left the husk behind.

"Go," I commanded, my voice low but absolute. "Move fast. We need to vanish before Frederic finds his footing."

The wolf flanked my side, hackles raised, his entire body quivering with tension. He padded in silence, his eyes ever scanning the shadows. We began our retreat, our footsteps echoing down ruined corridors that groaned around us like a wounded beast. The very walls seemed to close in, sagging beneath the weight of the secrets they held. There was magic here, rotting and old, clinging to the air like mildew on stone.

Dried blood painted sigils across the cracked flagstones. They whispered as we passed, voices from beyond the veil, echoing remnants of pain and madness and centuries of imprisonment. The kind of echoes you didn't answer if you wanted to keep your soul intact.

But I couldn't afford to listen. Not now.

Alice's weight leaned heavier into me with every step, her heat bleeding into my side. The way her body hung, half-conscious and unmoving, was a blade twisting in my gut but I pushed it down. There would be time to grieve, to rage, to fall apart.

Later.

Now, there was only forward.

Chester led us onward, a flickering orb of demonic

flame floating in his palm to guide our way. The light cast shadows that jittered against the walls, making the hallways ripple with movement that wasn't really there.

"The back stairwell's still intact," the demon muttered over his shoulder. "If we cut through the old wine cellar, Echo and I found a tunnel we can use. Leads beyond the perimeter."

"Good," I said. Even though nothing about this was good. Everything about this place screamed trap. Screamed unfinished business.

And part of me feared we hadn't escaped at all.

We were simply being let go, for now.

We turned a corner, and the air hit us like a wall. Thick, rancid, suffocating. A fetid mélange of blood, mildew, scorched flesh, and the acidic tang of old magic clung to the stone like rot. It wasn't just a scent, it was a presence, a living memory of carnage embedded in the foundation of this place. The corridor pulsed with a malignant resonance, as if the very walls remembered every scream, every curse, every drop of blood spilled in service of the twisted rituals wrought here.

Alice stirred faintly in my arms. A weak, incoherent groan vibrated against my collarbone. Her head lolled, her breath coming in shallow gasps. I bent down close, brushing her temple with my lips.

"You're alright," I murmured. "I've got you."

She didn't speak, but her hand twitched against my ribs somewhere between a grasp and a flinch. That was enough. Enough to tell me she was still fighting whatever terror they had done to her, even if just barely.

Behind us, the darkness shifted.

It was imperceptible at first, just the tiniest change in pressure, like the air being drawn inward. Then it grew;

Cold and aware. The sort of presence that didn't need to announce itself. It simply existed, as certain and terrifying as gravity.

Dominic stopped without a word. He stiffened, his head turning fractionally, his shoulders coiling with the silent tension of a predator who knew another had stepped into his domain.

"Keep going," I said softly, but even as I uttered it, I knew it for the lie it was. The pressure crawling up my spine, the frigid bite of instinct licking beneath my skin, whispered a different truth. Something, or someone, was there. Not attacking. Not chasing.

Watching.

"Him?" Echo asked, barely more than breath. Her fingers hovered near her dagger, magic gathering at her fingertips like condensation.

I didn't answer. I couldn't. Not with certainty. But I knew the scent of arrogance. I knew the quiet malice of something that enjoyed playing with its food.

Frederic wasn't dead. As much as I had longed to see him broken and ruined, he hadn't given us that satisfaction. No, he was alive. Perhaps wounded, perhaps biding his time but alive. And he had released us not out of mercy, but out of cruelty. He wanted us to run.

To think we'd escaped.

To hope.

Only so he could tear it all down again when the stakes were higher.

And that scared me more than a hundred Guardians at our backs.

"He's letting us go," I whispered. "Or thinks he is."

"For what purpose?" Chester muttered, flame still crackling in his palm as he glanced over his shoulder.

"If we get out of this place?" I exhaled, bitter. "Does it matter?"

The ancient stone staircase loomed before us, crumbling and slick with moisture. Echo ascended first, sure-footed despite the unstable setting. Chester followed close behind, his magical flame casting ghastly shadows along the walls, elongated, monstrous things that twisted as if trying to crawl back into the mansion's heart.

We moved in grim silence, the weight of what we'd endured pressing down as heavily as the unconscious bodies we bore. Dominic adjusted Rowan's limp form across his shoulders without complaint, though the witch hung like a broken marionette, his limbs swaying with each jarring step.

Alice's weight in my arms felt heavier now, not just physically, but emotionally. Her heat was growing, her skin nearly scalding. Whatever vile enchantment Frederic had left festering in her system hadn't abated. If anything, it was thriving.

She was burning from the inside out.

"We need to get her out," I said, my voice roughened by more than exhaustion. "Somewhere clean. Somewhere untouched by this cursed stone. We need to purge whatever he did to her before it consumes her completely."

"We will," Dominic said with quiet certainty. "But we can't help her from inside a crypt."

The moment we breached the upper tunnel—a dirt-walled corridor that reeked of damp moss and old blood—I felt a sliver of relief. Not safety. Not yet. But something close to breath.

The servant tunnels were narrow, the ceiling so low that Dominic was forced to stoop, and the walls were lined with brittle wooden beams and clawed-up stones. Roots had broken through the earth, curling along the walls, twisting deeper into the tunnel, splitting stone and wood as they went.

It felt like crawling through a corpse.

I pressed Alice closer, shielding her as best I could from the dripping ceiling and the grasping tendrils of the forest. Her fevered skin seared against mine, and I gritted my teeth to keep walking. Every instinct I had was screaming to stop. To set her down. To fix it. But we couldn't stop. Not here. Not yet.

Behind us, the mansion groaned. The sound rolled like thunder down the passage: a low, lingering wail of ancient wood and crumbling stone. The sound moved through the corridor in waves, low and thunderous, as if the very bones of the estate were cracking under the weight of its sins. It wasn't just decay we heard, it was despair. Centuries of blood-soaked rituals and suffering compressed into one final, echoing lament.

A house in mourning.

A predator denied its kill.

And still, I did not look back.

That place had already carved too much from our souls, each wall steeped in echoes, each step haunted by ghosts we hadn't yet named. Whatever power lingered there was ancient, bitter, and patient. If I turned, I feared it would remember my name.

We pressed forward, the air thick with dust and old wine. At last, we emerged into what remained of the mansion's lowest cellar, the remnants of the wine vault Chester had spoken of in a breathless hush back in the tunnels. Time had not been kind to it. Most of the vault had caved in, the collapse opening a gaping maw of broken stone and exposed dirt.

And there, beyond the wreckage, was salvation.

An earthen tunnel stretched outward like a lifeline, carved from desperation or divine mercy, I didn't care which. At its far end, thin daylight filtered in, a single silver ribbon smeared across the packed earth. It was a ghost of a promise. A breath of freedom.

Faint. Remote.

But real.

And it was enough.

"Almost there," Chester said, his voice hoarse as he extinguished the flame in his hand.

"Don't slow down now," I urged, shifting Alice again. She groaned softly, her lashes fluttering.

"Brooklyn…" she whispered, barely audible.

"I'm here," I said as my throat tightened. "You're safe. I've got you."

But even as the words left my mouth, I wasn't sure they were true. Because safety was an illusion. And war was only beginning.

Frederic hadn't let us go because we'd beaten him.

He'd let us go because now he knew exactly how far we would go for each other.

And he would use that.

He would exploit it.

And I would kill him for it.

With no hesitation. No mercy.

No looking back.

Chapter Twelve

DOMINIC

Rowan's weight pressed into my shoulders like penance.

He was light now. Too light. As if whatever Frederic had done to him had burned away everything solid, everything human in my friend. I shifted him carefully across my back, muscles straining, but I didn't complain. Couldn't. Not when the only sound behind us was the slow, groaning collapse of a place that had nearly devoured the people who counted on me to protect them.

The others moved ahead, Brooklyn clutching Alice to her side, her steps rigid with purpose. The wolf padded behind them, limping slightly, its muzzle still stained red. Chester and Echo scouted the path, flanking the tunnel like a pair of tired sentries. All of us were barely breathing.

But breathing nonetheless.

I should have felt relief. But it didn't come.

Instead, it sat heavy in my chest like smoke after a fire. The kind that seeps into your lungs and settles there, unshakable. Rowan hadn't stirred once since collapsing. Not even when his head bounced against my spine. His magic was silent. Too silent. Like someone had locked the doors from the inside and thrown away the key.

And Alice... She hadn't moved since we left the mansion. Her body sagged into Brooklyn's grip like an overfilled vessel trying to remember how to hold its own weight. Her skin was too warm. Her pulse too fast. And I could feel it, something still tangled inside her, like residual wires buzzing from Frederic's last attempt to tell me fuck you.

The bastard hadn't needed to chase us.

We delivered ourselves on a silver platter like he knew we would.

Whatever that fucker touched, he left poison in his wake.

And Brooklyn, gods, my mate, walked like she was made of steel, but I knew the truth. I knew the way her shoulder dipped just slightly when she carried too much weight in her soul. I saw the tremor in her fingers when she thought no one was watching. She was holding on by threads. Rage. Love. Sheer willpower. The female was a force to be reckoned with.

But even steel bends when it's heated enough.

I was afraid for all of them.

Beneath that fear, older and quieter, something else stirred—something I hadn't dare speak aloud.

Couldn't.

That presence back in the mansion. The one that didn't follow. Didn't attack. Only watched.

It hadn't felt foreign.

It had felt... familiar.

Not in the way an enemy feels familiar after too many battles. No. This had been intimate. Intrinsic. Like the echo of a dream I once lived or a shadow that had grown up alongside my own. Its attention had been sharp, specific, like it knew me. Like it belonged to me.

Or worse, like I belonged to it.

I swallowed hard, the weight of Rowan shifting as I adjusted my grip.

We broke through the tunnel mouth just as the car came into view, hidden beneath thickets and trees, half-sunken into the dirt like it had been holding its breath for our return. Brooklyn opened the back door and helped Alice inside, cradling her head with gentler hands than I'd seen her use in all the time I'd known her. I laid Rowan in the back as well, watching his chest rise in tiny, stuttering motions. It was a miracle he was still alive.

Chester started the engine. Echo sat up front, scanning the woods with that permanent scowl I'd noticed she wore when she was too focused. Brooklyn climbed into the back with me, and the wolf settled at our feet, growling low at nothing.

My mate grabbed my fingers, squeezing tight like she was too afraid to say anything until we were far away from here.

And me…

I kept staring at the tree line.

Because the feeling hadn't left.

That presence… it wasn't in the mansion anymore. It was here. Lingering. Just out of reach. Just out of sight.

And it wanted something.

From me.

The vehicle shuddered as Chester coaxed it into motion, tires crunching over gravel and moss-slick roots, the engine growling low like it too resented returning to the world of the living. Inside, the silence was unbearable, not the peaceful kind that soothed, but the taut, breathless hush that followed calamity and preceded grief.

The air was thick with exhaustion, with blood and sweat and the stench of something ancient we had disturbed.

I couldn't take my eyes off Rowan.

He lay as though carved from marble, pale and unmoving, lips tinged a worrying shade of gray. The faint rise and fall of his chest was the only thing keeping me from believing we were already too late. He had been my brother in arms, my confidant when I trusted no one else. We had bled on the same soil, fought through the same nightmares. And now... he was fading in my arms like breath in winter. I hadn't lied to Brooklyn when I told her he didn't betray us. He would never do that, there was no doubt in my mind.

I wanted to scream. To demand something of the world, of the gods, of whoever or whatever might be listening.

But I did nothing.

I held his wrist between my fingers as if the thread of life pulsing there might not slip away if I gripped it tightly enough.

Beside me, Brooklyn leaned against the door, Alice curled in her lap, looking fragile and half-formed. Her fingers ran absent-mindedly through Alice's hair, the way someone might touch a ghost to make sure it's real. Her face was calm but it was the calm of someone bracing for impact.

"She's burning up," she whispered again.

I shifted to see Alice more clearly. Her skin gleamed with sweat, her cheeks flushed with a sickly pink that did not look healthy. Her lips parted with shallow, rapid breaths. Whatever magic Frederic had seeded into her, it hadn't been purged. It still writhed beneath her surface, coiled and venomous. We'd escaped the mansion, but the battle wasn't over. I only hoped Samir would know what to do.

Brooklyn didn't cry. She never had. But I saw the tremble in her lower lip before she locked her jaw and hid it behind clenched teeth. I knew her pain like I knew my own. And it broke me in places I hadn't realized were still soft.

"She's strong," I said quietly, more for myself than for her. "She will fight it and win."

"She shouldn't have had to be strong, Dominic," Brooklyn said, and in those six words was a lifetime of fury and sorrow. "She should've never been in this position to begin with."

The trees blurred past the window, shadows and sun slicing in ribbons through the branches. But my mind wasn't in the car. It wasn't even in the forest. It was back in that crumbling house of horrors. And I had no idea what to tell my mate. Why did my thoughts linger back in that crypt of terror?

Back with the thing that watched us leave.

Its presence lingered in my marrow. Not like a memory. Not like fear.

Like blood.

It felt carved into me. Known. Intimate in the way a name is intimate when whispered against skin. It wasn't Frederic. It was something other. Something buried deep under all the magic and curse of that place.

A voice I couldn't hear, but could almost feel, whispering from the dark.

Find me.

See me...

I pressed my palm against the side of my skull, trying to scrub the sensation out of my brain.

Brooklyn glanced at me then. "You feel it too."

I nodded, not trusting myself to speak. She didn't press. She never did when I looked like this, like something was crawling just beneath the surface of my skin and trying to rip its way free.

The car bounced, tires slamming into a rut. Alice whimpered in her sleep. Rowan remained still.

"I don't think it was just watching us," I said finally. "I think it knew me. And not in the way enemies do."

Brooklyn tilted her head, the hard line of her jaw tight with thought.

"I didn't feel fear, not even for you," I admitted. "I should have. But I didn't. It felt... familiar. Like something that used to be mine."

She stared at me then, really stared, and for a second, I thought I saw something flicker across her face. Recognition. Dread. Possibility.

And then she looked away.

We were all carrying things we hadn't named yet. Burdens without language.

The trees began to thin. I recognized the ridge that crested before our hidden road. The safe house was close, another hour, maybe less. I should have felt relief. But all I felt was the weight of what came next.

Getting them safe wasn't enough.

Alice needed more than safety. She needed purging, cleansing, healing from magic none of us fully understood.

And Rowan... gods, I didn't know if he'd ever come back.

And then there was Brooklyn. My mate. My fire-forged soul.

She looked so calm. So fierce.

And yet I could feel the tremble in her spirit. The way she wanted to scream and couldn't. The way her rage was already planning ten different ways to destroy the man who'd hurt her family.

And I…

I was haunted by something that felt like me.

We were leaving one battlefield only to enter another. A slower one. A quieter one. But no less deadly.

As the car turned down the concealed path toward the safe house, I leaned back, closing my eyes for just a breath.

I did not sleep.

I listened to the echo of that familiar darkness still whispering inside me hoping to recognize it.

I waited for it to speak again.

Chapter Thirteen

BROOKLYN

Samir's house should have felt like sanctuary. A place where we didn't need to look over our shoulder.

But it didn't.

After the Council set up the attack not too long ago the place felt foreign. Unwelcoming. The walls were too still. The air too stale. The quiet pressed against my ears like a scream buried just beneath the surface.

Alice lay on the makeshift cot we'd dragged into the center of the common room, her skin too pale against the patchwork of blood-stained blankets reminding me of the similar scenario from a few weeks ago where she was fighting for her life in a similar fashion. I couldn't take her to her room because panic was clawing at my chest just thinking about everything she went through there. We also opened a circle like before, hoping that would trigger healing in her. So far nothing had changed.

Rowan was across from her on the couch, limbs tangled awkwardly, his chest rising in shallow, erratic gasps as Echo hovered beside him, whispering words beneath her breath that left red sigils dancing just above his clammy skin like fireflies. I wanted to feel bad for thinking he betrayed us but I had other, more powerful emotions trying to destroy me internally without it.

Chester paced near the windows, one hand idly tracing red glowing wards into the glass over and over as if that will protect us if the Syndicate decides to attack again. The sparks at his fingertips had long since gone out but he didn't stop, didn't so much as blink. Sheen glistened on his upper lip and droplets of sweat dribbled down his neck, but he didn't notice any of it. A silent, steady presence making sure we were ready if anything came our way.

Being down at the cages in that mansion unnerved all of them as I feared it would. They were very twitchy, almost paranoid now but I couldn't do anything to help them with that. I still fought my own nightmares from my time there.

Dominic crouched beside me, his fingers tangled in his hair as he watched Alice's face, for the thousandth time, for any type of sign. The wolf was here too, muzzle pushed close to Alice's arm, ears pinned to the back of his head, eyes as big as saucers, staring at her unblinking. There was no change. No twitch of her lips. No spark behind her eyelids. She was burning from the inside out with Frederic's poison, but none of us could name it, much less undo it.

And Samir…

After blanching when he saw us walking in with Alice draped over my arms and Rowan over Dominic's shoulder, he turned his back and disappeared without a word. A feeling I didn't dare name lodged itself in my chest at that. Now, he still hadn't come out of his room hours later.

"Samir," I called out softly, my voice thin from where I sat curled beside Alice's cot, knees drawn to my chest, forehead resting against the edge of the mattress. I knew he could hear me. "We need you. Alice needs you."

Silence.

Not even the rustle of movement from behind that damned door. It might as well have been a wall. All my hopes that he might have an idea of what we were facing suffered a sudden death the moment he closed that damn door with a very definite click.

Echo stilled, her hand hovering inches above Rowan's pallid forehead, the damp cloth trembling slightly between her fingers. Her silver gaze shifted sharply toward the dim hallway, shadowed by that heavy, impenetrable silence. The line of her jaw tightened, etched with restrained tension. "Something feels off," she said softly, her voice low and thoughtful, yet edged with unease. "Samir's never been this quiet since I met him. Not even in his darkest moods. He broods with intention, with sound and weight. There's a presence to it. But this?" She shook her head slowly, lips pressed into a line. "This is absence. A hollow. And that's not like him."

"He's not brooding, that's why," I said, unable to keep the edge out of my voice. "He's hiding."

That earned me a look from her. Sharp, assessing.

Dominic spoke before she could. "She's right," he murmured from where he sat beside Alice, one of her hands now gently clasped between his larger ones as if he could push life into her that way. His eyes never left her face like he was afraid that she would open her eyes and he would miss it. "I heard him pacing earlier. Light. Sneaky. He's still in there, in case you think he left without us knowing."

"But why not say anything?" Echo demanded, a line forming between her brows. "He knows what's happening. He knows they're both in trouble." A long stare at Alice made her forehead wrinkle more. "I thought he cared about the human."

Dominic finally looked up. His gaze was steady, but there was something stormy beneath it. "Because he's not ready to face us. To face Brooklyn. He's ashamed."

Echo narrowed her eyes. "Of what?"

"That's the question, isn't it?" I said. My tone had softened, but something inside me felt colder now. "Samir doesn't go silent unless there is something he doesn't want us to see. And right now? I think he doesn't want me to see that he's sinking in guilt."

Echo crossed her arms. "I don't presume to tell you what to do, Brooklyn, but if I were you, I would demand answers." She glanced pointedly at Rowen first then at Alice again. "Especially if my friends are suffering like this."

"You can't force someone to come clean before they're ready," Dominic said quietly. "And if you try, you won't get the truth, not with someone like Samir…You'll get lies, stories to justify one's actions. We don't need lies right now."

I looked at him, then at the hallway. At the closed door with no light beneath the crack. I'd tried knocking twice earlier. Echo had tried yelling through the wood, taunting him that he was scared of a little demon like her. Even Chester had made an attempt with all the subtlety of a battering ram. Still, Samir hadn't made a sound. Not even a peep.

"So, what do we do?" Echo stretched her arms above her head, cracking her neck and twisting this way and that to get some circulation in her limbs. The poor female had been hunched over Rowen since we placed him on that couch. "I tried everything I can think of but my magic is useless for either of them."

With one last look at Alice, I stood, brushing my palms

on my jeans, the movement stiff and reluctant. I didn't want to leave her here but I had no choice. "Samir is the last of my worries right now. We let him sit with whatever he cooked for himself. And if that's guilt, I hope he chokes on it before I do it for him. I'm done waiting for help that won't come. I need answers and I have every intention of finding them."

"Finding them where?" Echo asked.

"A reservation not too far from here," I said. "I'm going to see Laughing Crow." The name left my mouth like a vow. "She helped us once. She might do it again."

Echo blinked. "The shaman?"

"You know her?" Surprised that the demon spoke as if she was acquainted with the female, I eyed her warily.

Echo just blinked at me. The expression on her face more than conveyed what she thought about my question.

"She's more than just a shaman," I finally said, pushing away my curiosity. "She's one of the people Frederic fears. Main reason Alice took…" I trailed off, unwilling to share my weakness with the demons. They didn't need to know about the shifters we stashed in the reservations or the fact I probably won't be able to enter the reservation thanks to the said shamans and their wards.

Dominic, still holding Alice's hand, gave a slow nod of understanding when I threw him a desperate look. "If anyone can see through this… it's her. She helped Alice with you, maybe she will do the same for her."

"That's what I am hoping for, as well," I told him sincerely.

"I'm going with you." Dominic straightened as I expected him to do. "After everything that's happened, I'm not letting my mate out of my sight." That last part was for Echo and Chester's benefit.

I met Echo's suspicious eyes. "Stay with them. Watch Samir's door. Don't try to force him out but make sure he stays away from both of them. If he's going to talk, it has to be his choice. If not, I can always make him later."

Echo hesitated then nodded once. "It'll be my pleasure to put him in his place if he tries to touch either of them. But if he bolts while you're gone, I'm hunting him down myself."

"I will neither stop you nor hold that against you." I spoke loud enough that there was no doubt Samir heard it.

I took one last glance toward the silent door, my chest heavy with disappointment I didn't want to feel.

He was in there. Awake. Listening.

And hiding.

Like a damn coward.

From me.

From himself.

And that was something I couldn't deal with. Not now.

Not yet.

So, I turned and walked away, already thinking of the winding roads toward the reservation and the one female who might have the answers I so desperately needed.

Chapter Fourteen

BROOKLYN

The wind was cruel in the way only dusk winds are, neither warm nor cold, just persistent. It scraped over the land like a restless spirit, whispering through the brush, carrying scents of earth, ash, and something old. The reservation gate rose from the ground like a solemn sentinel, carved from aged cedar and etched with glyphs that pulsed faintly in the dying light. Wards shimmered across its threshold, an invisible veil humming with power.

And I couldn't cross it.

I stood there, only a few paces from the boundary, the very air thick with ancestral magic that repelled every step I might dare to take. My body tensed against it, like the bones in me understood this land would not welcome me unless invited. Even Dominic couldn't pass the wards since we had the mate link connecting us. Whatever magic the humans used recognized him as one of the Atua, one of my kind, because of me.

So, Dominic stood silently at my side. He hadn't said much since we'd left the others, or after he doubled over in excruciating pain when he tried to dart toward the gate. He didn't need to. His presence alone steadied me, kept the storm inside from ripping free and swallowing everything in its path. He understood why I was here—why I had to do this alone. And he didn't blame me for making him one of the unwanted at the reservations. If anything, he looked proud, carrying that quiet satisfaction that the magic had recognized him as my mate.

"Let them know who will be coming for them if they touch a hair on your head," he told me with his chest puffed up. If I was not emotionally, physically and mentally drained, I would've laughed until my sides hurt. This male was seriously something. So endearing. But I couldn't allow myself to enjoy it. To enjoy him.

I'd left Alice pale and burning, her breathing shallow and uneven. Rowan, even more ghost than male now, was barely holding on to life. And Samir, silent and locked away with his secrets, gave me nothing but more weight for my already overburdened shoulders.

I couldn't fix all of them. I wasn't a healer. But I could beg. And I could bleed if that's what it took to remedy what my presence in their lives had destroyed.

"I don't know if they'll let me in even if I ask," I murmured, my voice barely audible against the wind. My fingers flexed unconsciously at my sides, the phantom memory of Alice's limp weight still clinging to my skin. "They've never allowed anyone like me to step foot past this gate. And I don't blame them."

Dominic finally spoke, his voice low and steady. "Then we wait. If it takes hours, or days... we wait."

I turned to look at him, my eyes tracing his profile slowly. "Even if she's dying?" The words choked behind my clenched teeth.

He didn't blink. "Especially then. We do this right. Or not at all. You can't help Alice if you die. I will not allow it, Brooklyn. Don't ask it of me. I'm begging you."

I exhaled slowly. The patience and love in him could crush mountains, weather all storms. It made me ache with gratitude and fury at once. Because I wanted to break down the gate, tear through the wards with every ounce of rage and desperation I carried but that wouldn't bring them to our side. Dominic was right. If I do that, it would only confirm their fear of what I was.

So, I sat down in the red dust just outside the threshold, arms wrapped around my knees, eyes fixed on the path beyond. The land stretched out in golden silence, the grasses whispering secrets only the old souls could hear. Somewhere past the trees, the community waited, and beyond that was the shaman.

Laughing Crow.

The one shaman I had not only heard stories of, but seen, once, from a distance. A woman cloaked not in feathers or robes but in quiet strength, eyes sharper than bone knives, heart stitched with fire and water both. She owed me nothing. I could offer her nothing but a plea and the raw wound of my love for a friend. That must mean something.

The sky darkened inch by inch, draining the color from the world and pulling my strength back with it. I couldn't afford to wait for full night to reach the reservation, so I endured the sluggish crawl of fading daylight, holding out for that moment. Dominic crouched beside me, his shoulder brushing mine. Neither of us spoke. There was no need.

Time passed like a tide. Nothing moved.

Until a figure appeared at the far edge of the path.

A silhouette emerged at the edge of the path, framed in

the final copper light of the setting sun. At first, I thought it might be a shadow, a trick of desperation and dying light, but the figure moved with too much purpose, too much rooted weight. A man. Broad-shouldered, tall, his gait steady as he approached the gate.

Dominic stood at once, eyes narrowing protectively, but I lifted a hand without rising.

"Wait," I whispered. "Let him come."

The man stopped just beyond the boundary line, his gaze sweeping over the two of us. He wore no uniform, no symbols of power or rank. Just dark denim, worn boots, and a flannel shirt rolled at the sleeves. But there was something ancient in his presence. Something unyielding.

"You've been here a long time, Jumlin," he said, his voice low, unhurried. It had the cadence of stone warmed by sun, not unkind, but measured. I flinched at the insult. "You know you can't cross."

"I know," I said, quickly standing. Dust clung to my clothes, but I didn't care. "I'm not trying to. I just...I need to speak with someone." Swallowing thickly, I prayed he wouldn't walk away. "I need to speak with your shaman. With Laughing Crow."

At the mention of her name, his brows drew together slightly. Not a scowl, but more like the tightening of threads woven too many times before.

"Laughing Crow does not accept visitors like you."

"I wouldn't ask if it weren't life or death." My voice trembled. I hated that. I was used to fire, to fury. But this wasn't a battlefield I could win by force. "My friend...Alice. She's... she's dying. We tried everything. She's under a spell. Something unnatural, binding and burning her from the inside out. She won't make it through the night without help."

The man's expression didn't change. He simply watched me with eyes the color of scorched pine bark. Measuring. Weighing.

I stepped closer to the invisible line, just short of the ward's shimmer. Yet he still stood firm without any fear I could notice. "Please," I whispered. "I don't care if I have to wait out here all night. I don't care if she spits in my face when she sees what I am. Just let her know I'm here. Tell her Brooklyn asks for her mercy. That I'll owe her anything she asks."

Behind me, Dominic shifted his weight, silent but present. The muscles in his arms were taut, ready to spring if this turned, but still following my lead.

Still, the man said nothing.

"I've never been here before," I added quietly, desperation pressing at the back of my throat. "I've sent many that take sanctuary at your reservation but never asked for anything in return. I've never asked for help from your people. And I swear to you, I'm not lying. And if you don't believe me, look at me."

I lifted my hand and pressed it to my own chest, above my heart. "She's like a sister to me. I'm not asking for myself. Just for a chance to save her."

The man's gaze softened just slightly. Enough that I knew something had shifted.

He gave a short nod. "Wait here."

Then he turned and walked away, back into the shadows of the trees, his boots silent on the earth.

I sank to my knees, pressing shaking hands to cover my face.

"You think he'll come back?" I asked Dominic through my fingers.

My mate lowered himself beside me again, one arm brushing mine. "If he believed you... yes."

"And if he didn't?"

"Then we'll wait until someone else comes. Or until you fall asleep and I carry you home myself."

I laughed, dry and cracked. "You'd have to fight me first."

He didn't smile. "Then I'd fight you. I have a bad feeling about this, Brooklyn."

The last light faded from the sky, and the wards shimmered faintly like stars clinging to the soil.

I closed my eyes, and prayed to whoever listened that the shaman had humanity in her and at least heard my plea. I barely breathed from the tension coiling my muscles.

And waited...

And waited.

Chapter Fifteen

ALICE

There was no light here.

No ceiling.

No walls.

Just an endless, viscous dark pressing against my skin like oil. It clung to me, slow, suffocating, creeping into my nose, my throat, my lungs. Breathing felt like swallowing static.

Existing felt... optional.

I wasn't sure if I was dying.

Or if I had already died and just hadn't been informed.

Everything hurt. But not in the way a body hurts. Not flesh or bone. This pain was stranger. More intimate. Like my soul was being plucked apart string by string, tuned and snapped, over and over again.

It began in my core; A sharp, smoldering heat coiled like a serpent behind my ribs. It twisted tighter with each second that passed, unwinding only to tear through me again. I would've screamed if I could find my voice. But even that had been stripped away in this liminal void.

No chains here.

No dungeons.

No Frederic with his knife and smirk.

Only the remnants of his magic, buried so deep I felt it chewing at the marrow of what made me, me.

And inside it all.

Something else was moving.

Not the curse. Not the pain.

Me.

Or at least, a version of me that still remembered how to fight.

She stirred in the shadows, barefoot, bloodstained, wearing a cracked pair of glasses and a manic grin. She was the girl who once beat back demons with a crowbar. The girl who had nothing but bad jokes and rage and a promise to her best friend stitched across her ribcage like armor.

"You're not dead," she told me, her voice echoing weirdly in this not-space.

I stared at her. At myself.

"Could've fooled me," I muttered.

She cocked her head. "You're not dying either. Not yet. The magic's just... confused. Like a virus stuck in its own code."

"The virus is melting my brain."

She shrugged. "Then melt back harder."

There was a pause. The darkness rippled, and for a moment, I swore I heard Brooklyn's voice. Faint. Distant. Like wind through leaves.

It tugged at something deep inside. A tether I didn't know I still had.

"I told you she'd come," my shadow-self said. "Now all we have to do is not combust before she gets to us."

Easy.

Another pulse hit me, white-hot and merciless. It clawed

through my veins like molten metal. I arched, trembling in this bodiless existence, as the magic inside me howled. It wasn't trying to kill me anymore.

It was trying to take root.

Oh gods.

Was I being turned into a vessel?

Images flickered around me, flashes of glyphs, broken circles, the smell of burned sage and blood. I saw Frederic's sneer. Rowan's empty eyes. My hands lighting up with power that wasn't mine.

"No," I whispered. "No, no, no…"

"You can fight it," the other me said. "You've always been good at pretending. Pretend this isn't your mind. Pretend it's a lock. And break it."

I clenched my fists.

Somewhere beyond this mental prison, I knew my body still lay trembling. Fevered. On the brink.

But here?

I was still here.

And that meant I could fight.

Even if I didn't win. Even if I tore apart what was left of my mind doing it, I wouldn't hand over my body, my thoughts, my soul. Not to Frederic. Not to the curse. Not to anything.

I screamed.

Not out of fear.

But defiance.

And the darkness rippled.

Cracked.

Sharp pain speared through me, and I burst into a million pieces.

It was dark.

But not the kind of darkness that meant nothing.

This was a darkness that breathed. That pulsed. That listened.

I stood barefoot in a corridor that defied reality, endless and surreal, like a strip of forgotten film playing on a loop, its colors desaturated and its frames juddering. The walls swelled with each breath I took, as though the space itself was mimicking the fragile rhythm of my lungs. Beneath my feet, the ground beat like a heart...uneven, persistent, aching. Somewhere ahead, hidden in the shadows, something ancient loomed. Cold. Watching. Waiting.

The most disturbing part wasn't the impossible architecture or the way the air hummed like the breath of a sleeping beast. No, it was the sense that I'd been here before. Not in a dream. Not in memory. But in the marrow of my bones, in the hidden corners of my psyche.

This place wasn't unfamiliar.

It was intimate.

It was me.

Or what was left of me.

Magic throbbed beneath my skin, wild and foreign, running too hot and too cold in alternating waves. It didn't belong to me. It had a pulse all its own, slithering through my veins like a parasite with purpose, curling possessively around my bones like ivy made of knives. I could feel it whispering things I couldn't quite hear, a cacophony just below consciousness.

I wanted to scream.

To tear it out.

To demand it leave.

But my throat betrayed me, tight and silent, sealed under layers of fog and weightless pressure. My voice was buried too deep, sealed away like some forgotten secret. I opened my mouth, and nothing came out but the soundless press of desperation.

Still, I walked forward.

Because standing still meant surrendering.

And I didn't know how to do that. Not yet.

So, I walked. I had no choice.

Every step echoed with strange whispers, little chants in a language I didn't know but understood anyway. The words felt like needles. Ancient. Accusing. Familiar.

"Unworthy."

"Weak."

"Replaceable."

"She'll leave you next."

Brooklyn's name flared in my chest, a warmth amid the chill. That anchor. That tether. That one true goddamn thing. I clung to the feeling of her hand in mine. Not real, but real enough. If this place was trying to strip me of everything, it would have to pry that bond from my cold dead fingers.

And they were cold.

My fingers.

My arms.

My heart.

I stopped in front of a mirror. It stretched ceiling to floor, framed in black veins. My reflection smiled at me before I did.

"Oh no," I whispered. "No, no, no."

She was beautiful, the girl in the mirror. Too smooth. Too poised. Not me. Her eyes were molten gold, not brown. Her grin was all teeth and promise. Her voice was mine, but cracked open.

"You're unraveling," she said, tilting her head. "Finally."

I shook mine. "No. This isn't…"

"Real?" she offered. "It is. It's the only thing that is. The rest is borrowed time. You're a house built on someone else's blueprints. But me? I'm the foundation. The root. The truth. You just haven't let go yet."

She reached for me, palm to mirror, like she wanted to climb out.

I backed away, breath catching.

Magic coiled in my gut again, this time surging like it wanted to answer her call. I choked. It hurt. My knees gave way and I crumpled to the ground, hands fisting the illusion of carpet.

"Why are you fighting?" she asked, kneeling in the mirror now, eyes soft. "Wouldn't it be easier to stop and become what you were meant to be?"

Because of Brooklyn.

Because of Dominic.

Because of all of them.

I wanted to scream it, but no voice came out when I opened my mouth.

I was more than a vessel. More than a crack to be filled.

"No," I whispered. "You don't get to take my life from me. Not after everything."

The girl in the mirror frowned. "Then I'll have to burn it out."

The walls caught fire.

Magic surged through me again, this time tearing. Splitting. My body convulsed in this dream-space like it was caught in a live wire. I screamed, soundless, but the fire didn't touch me.

Something else did.

A memory.

Brooklyn's shy barely there smile.

Dominic's quiet strength.

Echo rolling her eyes.

Chester grinning at nothing.

Rowan's awkward, beautiful silence.

Samir's smoldering gaze on me when he thought I wasn't watching.

The soft fur and calming presence of my dog that I refused to call wolf.

They were light.

And I was not alone.

The mirror cracked.

So did the girl inside it.

"You're not strong enough," she hissed.

"I don't have to be," I said, rising to my feet even as my legs trembled. "I'm not doing this alone."

The fire died.

The walls split.

And for the first time since I'd arrived in this hell, the darkness retreated.

I didn't wake.

Not yet.

But I was close.

I'd be damned if I let Frederic win, that asshole.

He'd picked the wrong girl to mess with.

Chapter Sixteen

DOMINIC

The sky had surrendered fully to night, soaked in ink, stars like silver needles pricking through velvet black. Brooklyn hadn't moved in over an hour, though I knew the dusk had returned her strength. She sat curled at the base of the gate, arms wrapped tightly around her knees, eyes locked on the path ahead as if sheer willpower could summon the shaman from thin air. The wards shimmered faintly before her, their glow strained and unsteady, stretched to the limit.

I stood behind her, quiet, unmoving. A sentinel in the dark. The air was brittle with silence, and something about it frayed the edges of my instincts. My panther paced beneath my skin, restless, teeth bared in anticipation. I fought to hold him back; my language faltered in that form, and I needed to speak. But the line between man and beast had begun to blur.

I sniffed the wind. There was something foreign threading the air now, like iron and ash. Something that didn't belong to this place or its people. Unease prickled my skin.

Then the sound hit.

Footsteps. Dozens.

I turned just as they emerged from the tree line across the road, so many of them, moving with eerie precision, as if summoned by some silent command. One by one they stepped out of the shadows, their presence coalescing like a storm front made of flesh and menace. Men, or something close enough to wear their shape. Tall, impossibly broad-shouldered, their skin stretched taut over sculpted muscles that glistened under the silver wash of moonlight.

They were shirtless despite the cutting wind, clad only in black leather pants and harnesses that wrapped their torsos like restraints rather than armor. Not a sound passed between them. Not the rustle of breath, not the scuff of boot or the crack of twigs beneath their weight. Just that dreadful stillness, broken only by the slow, synchronized pace of their advance.

Their eyes glowed faintly blue, unnatural and cold, like the last flicker of a dying flame. Not vibrant, not alive but dimmed, dulled, as if whatever spark of will they once had had been stripped away and replaced with something... hollow.

I took a step back, instinct prickling along every nerve. These weren't Guardians. Not truly. They were too clean. Too perfect. No scent of blood, no flicker of thought. Just constructs wearing flesh. And I couldn't smell them.

"Brooklyn," I said quietly, placing myself between them and my mate while my animal thrashed under my skin.

She didn't need more. She was on her feet before her name left my lips.

The Guardians or whatever they were closed in fast. Too fast. They moved in perfect sync, not like soldiers but puppets. Controlled. Manufactured. Each footstep landed with the same weight. Each hand held the same curved blade, gleaming despite the darkness.

My hackles rose. My panther stirred behind my ribs, already pacing for release.

"They're not Guardians," Brooklyn hissed. "Something… Something's wrong."

Wrong was an understatement. Their magic reeked of precision. Synthetic. Not the brutal, volatile wildness that marked most Guardians. This was laced with illusion, suggestion, mimicry. A spell made to look like them.

But not feel like them.

Still, we couldn't afford a mistake. Not if they were real.

"You take the right; I'll take the left side," she said sharply, drawing her favorite blade from her thigh. "Don't let them corner us."

I shifted before I could speak, bones breaking, fur tearing through skin. In seconds I was down on four legs, muscle rippling, claws carving shallow trenches in the dirt. I let the beast take over, but only just. My mind stayed sharp, tethered to hers.

They struck first.

Brooklyn blocked one blow, ducked a second, then slammed her blade through the chest of the first Guardian to reach her. It split apart, not with blood, but smoke unraveling in moonlight.

An illusion.

But the next three came without hesitation.

I lunged, jaws sinking into the arm of one, but it dissolved in my mouth, leaving only the taste of burnt sage and bitter root. The scent of spellwork. I turned, dodging a strike, slashing across the belly of another. Again, smoke. Again, not real.

"They're testing us," Brooklyn said through clenched

teeth, spinning and slicing through another three. "This isn't an attack...it's a damn test."

"For what?" I growled, voice ragged through my half-shifted throat.

"To see if we meant what we said." She panted. "To see if I'm truly not like the rest of my kind." Her tone was laced with disgust.

Another wave came. I tackled two at once, twisting midair, ripping through what wasn't flesh. Brooklyn danced through the chaos like a storm; Elegant, brutal, relentless. Her blade left arcs of black light behind it. Her eyes glowed not just with rage, but conviction. The Guardians might not have been real and they turned to smoke when we landed a hit but we were real. Everywhere their blades touched opened our skin and blood poured from the wounds.

And then, just like that, the Guardians vanished.

Smoke. Ash. Gone.

Silence fell.

Brooklyn stood in the center of the clearing, chest heaving, silver blade covered with nothing but moonlight. Her eyes searched the trees, her power still thrumming like an exposed wire. Blood dripped from under her sleeve where a particularly deep cut was still oozing. I shifted back immediately and rushed to check her injuries.

Scrape of a boot over gravel alerted us to another presence.

Then, from the path beyond the gate, the man returned.

Unscathed.

Expression unreadable.

He regarded us for the longest time, then stepped forward just enough that we could see the glint of something ceremonial hanging from his neck. A carved wooden pendant shaped like a crow's talon.

"You fought," he said calmly. "But you did not kill." Suspicion laced his words and glinted in his dark eyes.

Brooklyn's voice was a low rasp as she wiped sweat from her forehead with the bloody sleeve of her shirt, marking her face like with war paint. "There was no one to kill. But, I hope I bleed enough to prove myself to you."

He nodded once, a small smile tugging on one side of his lips.

"You may speak with Laughing Crow now."

He'd barely finished the sentence when the wards parted for her like mist before moonlight.

I had no idea what I was expecting but it was rather uneventful after all the drama with conjuring spells and everything else.

There was no sound, no thunderous snap of magic, no chorus of ancestral judgment. Just the subtle unraveling of an invisible thread as the man nodded and gestured for us to follow. Brooklyn stepped forward, and the air bent around her. I followed on instinct, shadowing her movements without hesitation, my muscles taut, still riding the edge of a shift I hadn't fully decided was a good idea or not. We played our card. If they didn't know I was a shifter, they knew now.

And, it wasn't trust in the land that made me go after my mate. It was trust in her. Where she walked, I followed. I will willingly walk into death to follow her.

But, the moment I stepped past the boundary, the air thickened. Power hung like smoke in this place, woven into the very dirt under our feet. It pressed against my skin, curious like a child yet, ancient, older than the roots of the trees. It felt like walking into the mouth of a great beast that hadn't decided yet whether it wanted to feast.

Brooklyn said nothing, but I saw the tightness in her jaw,

the way her fingers brushed the handle of her blade not out of threat, but caution. This was sacred ground. She knew that, she respected it enough to not draw a weapon. And for all her fury, all her anxiety, she treated it as such.

We followed the man down a winding path lined with cedar and the gnarled trunks of trees so old they seemed fossilized. Puddles of old water were sprinkled on all sides, our boots splashing through them occasionally. Symbols carved into the barks glowed faintly, not bright enough to see clearly, but enough to feel like we were being watched. Judged.

And then they appeared.

The first wolf emerged like a whisper from between two trees, silent, massive, fur dark as charred earth. Its eyes gleamed with recognition, not aggression. Then another appeared. Then another.

Within seconds, we were surrounded.

Not wolves, shifters.

A whole pack of them lined up one side of the road then the other, all their eyes locked on my mate.

I slid closer to Brooklyn instinctively, my hand tightening into a fist, every muscle in my body ready to fight but they didn't move toward us. They circled, yes. But not like hunters. More like a congregation showing respect.

No growls. No baring of teeth. Only silent acknowledgement.

"What the hell...?" I murmured, glancing around.

"They remember," the man said simply, not turning to face us. His voice carried like it was bouncing off a canyon wall. "They were Syndicate targets once. Until she freed them."

I stared at the wolves again, now recognizing the differences between them, the color of their fur, the subtle shade of their eyes. These weren't just any shifters. They had been weapons once. They had fought against the Council and I believed them to be dead. And she had let them go.

"You saved them." I said to my mate. A statement, not a question.

She didn't answer at first. Just stared at the wolves, her expression unreadable. Then she said, very quietly, "I gave them a choice. That's all. I didn't know if they'd survive."

The silver-gray wolf, the largest, stepped forward and lowered his head to her. Not in submission. In reverence.

My breath caught. Not because of the gesture, but because of what it meant. I had always known Brooklyn was feared. I had always known she was powerful. But this… this was different.

She wasn't feared here. She was honored.

The wolf's gaze flicked to me, and for one suspended second, it felt like he was measuring me not just as her mate, but as a being. And then he dipped his head ever so slightly.

"Good for you. You're marked by her," the man said, glancing at me now. "The land knows it. The wolves know it, too."

That truth sank deep. Not just into my ears, but into my bones. I wasn't just with Brooklyn. I was bound to her, claimed not only in body, but in presence. And whatever magic lived in this place, it could see that.

Warmth spread through my chest, and I had to hold myself back so I didn't take my mate into my arms. "You're saying they trust me… because I am her mate?"

"I'm saying," he said, voice like roots cracking stone, "they won't tear you apart. Because she won't like that." A smirk grew on his smug face and I debated for a split second if I should wipe it with my fist.

Before I could do something entirely too stupid, he

gestured toward a structure ahead. A low, cedar-framed house, its windows glowing softly from within. Smoke drifted up from a chimney, carrying the scent of juniper and something older. Protective wards were carved directly into the lintel, sharper, more personal than the ones at the boundary gate. Not mass deterrents. Personal defenses.

We reached the fence and the closed gate. The man knocked once on it.

It opened.

She stood there, shorter than I expected. Braids laced with feathers and bone, a robe of layered wool and dusk-colored fabric that didn't cling, but flowed with a weight of purpose. Her face was lined by age, but not weakened by it. Her gaze struck me harder than any blow I'd ever taken in a fight. Eyes so dark there was no pupil to be seen accessed Brooklyn from head to toe.

Laughing Crow.

Her name felt too small for the presence in front of us. She didn't look at me first. Her eyes locked on Brooklyn like twin daggers unsheathed.

"She came," the man said behind us.

Laughing Crow didn't move. Didn't smile. Didn't speak. Her presence was like standing in front of a storm, still, but brimming with coiled energy.

Then, after an eternity, she stepped aside.

"Enter," she said. Her voice was smoke over stone. "And speak your truth. But know this. If you lie, you will not leave the way you entered."

Brooklyn nodded and walked past the threshold like a queen entering her trial.

And I followed.

As always.

I will go to death for my mate.

Chapter Seventeen

BROOKLYN

To say I was unprepared for stepping into the shaman's home would be the understatement of the damn century.

The moment my foot crossed the threshold, something ancient stirred, like a knife pressed gently to the underside of my ribs. Not a threat, exactly. Not yet. But a warning. Some primal instinct, buried so deep in my bones it predated language, snapped to attention, hissing like an animal too long caged.

With herculean effort, I smothered it. Wrestled it down where it writhed beneath my skin.

But she saw.

Of course, she did.

Laughing Crow's eyes, too black, too wide, like obsidian moons carved into the hollows of her face tracked my every twitch. She didn't speak. Didn't move. Just watched as my feet faltered on the threshold and my fingers curled instinctively before I forced them still.

"Which way?" I asked, hoping she'd walk ahead so I

could study her back instead of feeling her eyes scour mine like truths being etched from bone.

She didn't answer. Just tilted her chin toward the narrow hallway pulsing with warm light.

Subtle, clear. I didn't miss the message. *You know where to go. Go.*

And fine. She wasn't wrong. The direction was obvious. I just didn't like her witnessing my every misstep like she was tallying my worth in real time.

I swallowed my pride and stepped forward. The house groaned softly under my boots, the floorboards old, well-loved, and not altogether welcoming. The scent of sage and juniper hung thick in the air, masking something older. Smoke. Iron. Memory.

Dominic followed a step behind, steady as ever, his presence the only thing keeping me from unraveling into a thousand threads. But if I expected the shaman to acknowledge him, I was mistaken. She gave him only a flick of her gaze and nothing more.

No, her attention remained solely on me. A scalpel gaze. Watching not just what I was, but what I carried.

"I didn't come here to start trouble," I said quickly, ducking beneath a hanging bundle of dried thyme strung from the ceiling like a ward.

The kitchen we entered was sparse and weathered, more function than form. The walls bore the kind of dust that carried generations, not neglect. Mismatched furniture lined the space; A rocking chair in the corner cloaked in a faded quilt, gently swaying in an unseen breeze like some ghost was still lounging there.

"I wouldn't have stepped foot on your land if I wasn't desperate," I continued. "This wasn't a decision made lightly."

"Yes, yes," she muttered, waving one hand like she was shooing off gnats. "You're all desperate when you come to me. Always on the verge of ruin. Alice was no different."

Her voice sank into my spine like a thorn, and I halted mid-step.

"What?" I asked, turning my head slowly, narrowing my eyes.

She snorted, unfazed. "The two of you are carved from the same troublewood. Always running toward fire and then crying when you get burned. Maybe if you both made less spectacularly bad choices, you'd require less... assistance."

I bit back my retort.

The shaman drifted across the room with a grace that defied age. She didn't walk so much as glide, her bare feet silent against the old pine floor. Every movement carried authority, measured, exact. Like nature didn't dare defy her.

A feline shape curled on the rocking chair stirred, a soot-colored cat who, upon laying eyes on me, instantly bristled. Her spine arched into a perfect crescent, green eyes slitting into knives. She hissed, lashing her tail like a whip behind her.

Until she spotted Dominic.

Then all hell broke loose.

Her pupils dilated, and she loosed a low growl like she was ready to summon the wrath of Bast herself. And Dominic, my ever-so-dignified mate, hissed back. Full lips peeled back over fangs in a snarl so primal I flinched.

The cat bolted.

Straight between us like a shot, claws skittering on wood, gone before I could even swear properly.

"Really?" I asked flatly, turning toward him. My voice was dry enough to start fires.

He just shrugged, utterly unrepentant. "She started it."

"She's a cat."

"A disrespectful one."

"Felines of any kind," Laughing Crow said mildly, amusement dripping like honey from her lips, "are strange creatures—moody, territorial, dramatic. Little assholes. Especially with their own kin."

She gestured toward two wooden chairs pulled up near the center of the room, her black eyes dancing with mirth. "Sit. Or hiss some more at each other, but preferably somewhere I don't have to bless again."

Her gaze lingered pointedly on Dominic, who arched a brow in that lazy, warning way he had. He didn't like being dismissed, let alone mocked, but he was smart enough to pick his battles.

I jumped in before the situation could combust. "He's aware of his assholish behavior," I rushed to say, dragging a chair backward and collapsing into it before the situation got any weirder.

Dominic's mouth twitched. Whether in amusement or protest, I couldn't tell. But he remained standing behind me, arms crossed, eyes fixed on Laughing Crow like he didn't entirely trust her not to turn him into a worm.

Wise, honestly.

She poured herself a measure from the soot-blackened kettle, steam rising in faint curls that drifted toward the ceiling. Then, without a word, she poured a second cup and offered it to me.

The clay mug was warm, no, *hot*, and the scent struck like a warning: pungent sage, scorched yarrow, and something darker beneath it. Bitter and old. Like regret, distilled.

She did not ask if I wanted it.

"You came for my help," she said at last, her voice low and unhurried, yet sharper than my blades. "For your Alice.

The girl who nearly knocked over three generations of my grandmother's pottery while bleeding on sacred stone."

I flinched despite myself. "Yes." The word slipped out smaller than I intended. Too humble. Too raw.

The truth was, I had nothing polished left in me. No argument prepared, no clever plea. Just desperation curled tight behind my ribs.

Laughing Crow took a slow sip from her cup and studied me with those wide, dark eyes that seemed to look through skin and bone to whatever soul might still remain. She did not blink. She did not sit. She merely stood there, childlike and quiet, like the storm that hadn't broken yet.

"Then tell me," she said eventually, tilting her head just so in a birdlike manner. "As much as I've been dying to meet you…Why should I offer aid to someone like *you*?"

Her words were not cruel. Not even scornful. Just… factual. Precise. And devastating.

I tightened my grip on the cup, grounding myself in the warmth. "Because I am willing to pay any price for her life," I said, voice steady even though I felt anything but. "Because I've watched her fight for others long after she had nothing left for herself. Because I would bleed out in this kitchen, on your ancestral floor, if it would buy her one more chance to live. If anyone deserves to be saved, that's Alice."

"And what," Laughing Crow asked, tone sharpened by something colder now, "makes her life more sacred than the thousands of others your kind have taken?"

I swallowed hard. "Nothing," I said. "Not a damn thing, yet here I am begging for your help."

That seemed to catch her attention.

"I'm not asking for forgiveness for my kind," I contin-ued. "Not from you. Not from the land. I know what I've done. What I *am*. You feel it in your bones…I don't belong here. I'm poison to your soil and your air and your wards. But Alice… Alice *does* belong. She chooses kindness always. She chose hope. Even when it nearly killed her. I didn't drag her into this. She walked with me willingly because that is who she is. And I would damn myself ten times over to save her from the consequences of that choice."

A long pause followed.

Her stare didn't soften, but something behind it shifted. The air grew heavier, like the room itself was listening.

"So," she murmured. "You offer your blood. Your life. To pay a debt if needed."

I nodded once. "Willingly."

"And what if the cost is not yours to bear?" she asked, her voice turning quiet as snowfall. "What if the price falls on *her*? Or worse, what is the payment is asked at a later date, unexpectedly, costing you something or someone you are not willing to part with?" her gaze flicked for a split second to Dominic and back. If I was not watching her like a hawk I would've missed it.

That struck like a knife between my ribs. I searched her gaze for any inkling that she was messing with me but something ancient stared back. "Then at least I will know she was given a choice at life. She can decide if she wants to pay or not. I will decide how to deal with whatever is asked of me, as well. For now? She will get help. Not death disguised as mercy."

Laughing Crow exhaled slowly, setting her mug down without a sound.

"You speak with pain," she said. "But not just for her. You speak with shame. With the guilt of one who has tasted ruin and dared to ask for something better."

I didn't answer. There was nothing left to say. I had no

defenses to offer, no lies, no shields, no claws. Only the jagged, bloody truth laid bare before her. I was a monster. She knew it. I knew it.

The land knew it, too.

Another long silence stretched between us.

Then, with the same unhurried grace as before, she turned and gestured toward the hallway.

"Come," she said. "You'll help me prepare the circle."

I blinked. "You're agreeing to help?"

"I'm agreeing to listen," she corrected. "And that's more than most like you have ever received."

Then, just as she stepped out of view, she added over her shoulder, "And if your friend lives… it will not be because you begged well. It will be because something in the bones of the earth answered for you."

Dominic reached for my hand from behind me. I didn't realize how hard I was trembling until our fingers met.

It took a long moment before I felt comfortable to stand up without worrying that my knees would give out and I'd collapse. But with each step I took to follow the shaman, I was certain that all our lives were about to change forever.

Chapter Eighteen

DOMINIC

The ground felt different here.

Not just beneath my feet, but beneath my skin. Beneath the bones. The deeper we moved into the back yard where Laughing Crow had prepared the ceremonial circle, the more it felt like something ancient stirred in the marrow of the world, like the earth itself was holding its breath.

I stood behind Brooklyn as the shaman began her slow circuit around the space, her bare feet whispering over the packed red earth, trailing smoke and quiet fire. Bundles of sage, cedar, and sweetgrass burned in low iron bowls at the corners, the scent thick and sharp, clinging to the inside of my nostrils.

She moved clockwise, invoking the elements one by one, and with each invocation, gooseflesh bloomed along my arms like a silent warning. Something ancient stirred: subtle, reverent, and watching.

"To the East," she intoned, her voice steady, resonant, full of something older than human memory. "Air and thought, the mind that dreams, the voice that cries out. I summon thee. Please enter."

A current of wind slipped into the clearing, sudden and deliberate, rustling the hanging herbs at the edge of the circle and tousling Brooklyn's hair. It wasn't natural. It didn't belong to the forest. It had been summoned.

"To the South, fire and will, the burning truth, the fury that births change. I summon thee. Please enter."

The flames in the bowls flared in response, tongues of orange and blue licking the edges of the iron. They didn't consume the herbs, only danced higher, flickering with awareness. As though the fire itself was listening.

"To the West, water and memory, the blood of the old ones, the mirror of all that was. I summon thee. Please enter."

The air thickened, turning damp like rain had kissed the soil minutes ago. A chill traced the edges of the circle, curling against my skin. I could feel moisture gather beneath my tongue, the ghost of river and salt and old grief rising with it.

"To the North, earth and silence, the grave and the womb, the stone that watches but never forgets. I summon thee. Please enter."

And then, the stillness. Heavier than silence. Complete. Not even the wind dared breathe. It was as if the earth itself held its exhale, waiting.

The world hushed.

And then, Laughing Crow stepped to the center.

Not hurried. Not hesitant. With the deliberate grace of someone who had done this a hundred times under a thousand stars. Her bare feet kissed the soil as if greeting kin. Her spine was impossibly straight, arms spread slightly from her sides, as though ready to embrace or strike or weep, depending on how the Great Spirit answered.

Around her, the circle seemed to tighten, unseen cords drawing in. The flames no longer danced, they held still, like sentinels. The wind no longer stirred. The damp remained, clinging to the edge of every breath like a web.

She tilted her head back, eyes open to the cosmos above, and began to speak, not in English, not in any language I knew. It was older than syllables. A rhythm. A resonance. Something the blood understood even if the brain couldn't translate.

It struck me then how small I was. How small we all were in the face of this.

Brooklyn stood just beyond the center, her posture still as death, her shoulders squared against whatever came next. She wasn't trembling, but I was. My panther coiled like a loaded spring beneath my skin, the hair on my arms and neck rose, not in fear but in awe.

Something was coming.

And that something wasn't known for mercy.

The shaman was calling to the Great Spirit. The force that bound all this together. Not to command. Not even to request. Only to be heard. To be considered.

The clearing where Laughing Crow had drawn her circle felt removed from time itself. Hidden deep within the heart of the reservation's sacred grove, the air carried weight—thicker, more viscous, as though time itself slowed just enough for the ancestors to linger between heartbeats. Massive stones stood at uneven intervals along the edge of the circle, their surfaces worn with carvings nearly swallowed by the centuries. Lichen clung to them, remnants of prayers too old to be forgotten.

The trees bowed inward, not just leaning with age but with intention as though they watched, listened, and judged. Their branches twisted into sigils that caught the moonlight in a thousand tiny eyes. The sky above was unnaturally clear, stars cast in high relief against the velvet black, as though the heavens themselves leaned closer to see what would unfold here tonight.

The fire crackled with unnatural rhythm, too measured, too even, as if it, too, had been called to order by Laughing Crow's hand. Around it, the air danced in strange currents now. Not from wind. Nor from magic. It was something else. Something other. A breath drawn by the world before it decided whether to speak.

Brooklyn stood in the center of the circle now, unmoving, her face unreadable, her spine rigid. I hadn't even seen her step forward. Her hand hung at her side, fingers twitching from the effort it took not to tremble. I knew her well enough to understand what it cost her to stand there in silence, to hold back the scream she wanted to let loose, to resist the urge to act when waiting alone wasn't enough.

She would pay any price for Alice.

That truth radiated from her like smoke off a battlefield.

But I...fuck, I didn't know if I could bear to watch her bleed for it.

I clenched my jaw, feeling the sting of my own helplessness settling in deep, iron-clad around my heart. If Laughing Crow asked for something unreasonable...if she dared ask for Brooklyn's life in exchange, or her power, or her soul...I didn't know if I could just stand here and let it happen.

I wanted to be the male who respected my mate's choices.

But I was also the mate who would burn this entire goddamn reservation to ash before I watched her die.

That fracture lived in my chest, widening with every breath.

I'd never been good at standing still while the people I love suffered. I was a creature of movement, of instinct, of violent solutions. I wasn't made for ceremonies and soul-rending bargains. I was made for teeth and claw. For protecting what I considered mine. For blood if needed.

She'd never forgive me if I intervened. I knew that. Her fury was a living thing, and I'd be the target if I stepped in, if I snapped the shaman's neck before a price could be named.

But I'd take her hate over her absence.

Every time.

My fingers twitched at my sides. My panther was pacing beneath my skin, crouched low in the background, ears flat, tail lashing. The animal didn't understand restraint. He knew only this: our mate stood at the center of a sacred circle, and we were outside it.

Powerless.

He didn't like it.

Neither did I.

Across the firelight, Laughing Crow's voice grew louder. She spoke to something I couldn't see, a ripple in the veil between worlds. I could feel it though. A presence gathering just out of reach. Not like a person stepping into a room but like a storm looming just out of sight, measuring whether we were worth the rain.

Brooklyn lifted her head at last and looked up into the dark, into the wind and stars and firelight. Her voice was steady when she spoke, even though I knew she was fraying inside.

"Great Spirit," she said. "If you hear me… hear not for my sake, but for hers. For Alice."

Her voice cracked just a little on the name.

"If there's a debt to be paid, let it fall to me. Not to her. If I have to give my life, I will. Gladly. But help her. Please. Break whatever curse was placed around her soul. Free my friend, I'm begging you."

I took a step forward.

Couldn't help it.

She didn't turn to look at me. She didn't need to. Her presence thrummed against mine through the bond, a quiet echo: Stay back. Let me do this.

"Name your price." My mate breathed, bracing for whatever came at her.

Gods, she was so fucking brave.

Too brave.

If the shaman turned now and demanded her soul, I knew exactly what would happen.

I would shift.

I would kill.

I would tear down this entire sacred forest if I had to.

I didn't care if it meant every wolf, every elder, every soul here turned on me.

I would not watch her die for anything.

Let her hate me later. Let her scream and call me a monster. Let her leave me if she had to.

But at least she'd still be breathing.

Because I could survive her fury.

I couldn't survive a world without her in it.

The fire flared suddenly, white-hot and unnatural, consuming all color for the briefest heartbeat of time.

Brooklyn dropped to her knees.

And everything…Everything went quiet.

My heart slammed once, hard against my ribs.

And I waited for the price.

For the answer.

For the moment I'd have to make the choice to let destiny decide our fates and take its toll…

…or destroy everything because of whatever it asked.

Chapter Nineteen

BROOKLYN

The circle felt alive.

Not metaphorically, but truly alive. As though it had lungs and breath and blood pumping through arteries sewn into the soil. The very air within it trembled with a presence I couldn't name, but felt in my marrow. Gooseflesh bloomed across my arms as Laughing Crow completed the last invocation and stepped into the center of her ancestral magic.

Something shifted the instant she crossed that invisible threshold. It was like stepping into the eye of a storm. No chaos, no sound, just stillness so profound it bordered on violent.

The flames around the bowls did not sway in the breeze. They held perfectly still, glowing bright as stars but casting no shadows. The air was damp and warm and ancient. Like memory had seeped into the very bones of the earth and gathered now to watch me.

Terrified of what it may see... A monster? Someone unworthy maybe? I tried hard not to dwell on that thought. I didn't know what I expected. Pain, maybe. Judgment. A voice booming from the sky to call me what I was a cursed thing, a half breed monster who dared beg mercy from forces far older than she understood.

But nothing came. Nothing except the pulse of power stretching outward in every direction.

Laughing Crow stood a few paces from me, her black eyes sharp, unreadable, rimmed with the reflection of the flames. She was silent, but her expression was no longer purely wary. There was something else beneath the lines of her face now. Something like curiosity. Or perhaps grief.

"Do not lie in this place," she said softly, voice barely louder than a whisper. A thick silver strand fell over one side of her face making her expression mysterious and chilling. "It will unravel you faster than any blade."

I nodded once. "I won't."

Her gaze lingered on me a moment longer before she knelt, laying her palms gently to the dirt at her feet. Her eyes closed. She didn't speak in words at first. Only in breath.

One inhale. One exhale.

Then she whispered, not in English, but in something older. Something raw. Her tongue shaped syllables that pulled at the lining of my skull, vibrating in the hollows of my chest. I couldn't understand the words, but my body did. My blood did.

The language of spirits. Of bones.

Smoke coiled from the firebowls as if summoned, curling into shapes that didn't make sense. Feathers, teeth, rivers, wounds. My mouth was dry as dust. I could feel Dominic just beyond the circle's edge, his presence taut with the kind of tension that preceded bloodshed. He would never interfere, but I knew what it cost him to stay still.

The chant rose, a crescendo of elements spun into harmony, and the temperature dropped again.

Laughing Crow opened her eyes.

And looked at me.

"The Great Spirit hears your plea," she said, her voice no longer fully hers. Something deeper rode beneath it, something that was chewing on the words like it didn't know what to do with them. Like they were foreign. "You offer your life in exchange for your sister's."

I nodded, heart stuttering. "Without hesitation." For whatever was lurking underneath the shaman's skin spoke the truth. Alice was my sister in all things but blood.

The wind shifted.

Louder now. Not angry. Not hostile. But attentive.

Listening.

"Why?" she asked, her tone laced with suspicion just as before. But this time the question did not come from her alone. It echoed, dissonant, layered. As if a chorus of voices from beneath the soil and above the stars demanded an answer.

"Because she saved me," I whispered, throat tight. "Not just from death. But from myself. Because she never looked at me like I was a weapon. A monster. Or a tragedy. She saw me as something worth seeing. Something good."

I took a step forward, toward the center.

"She chose me when she didn't have to. And I would burn down every version of myself before I let her die because of it."

The flames blazed brighter. The circle of energy surrounding us shimmered, pulses of light running through the ground like veins in stone.

Laughing Crow's breath caught and it was the first time I'd seen her startled.

"You would offer your life," she murmured, "to the earth. To the old powers. Knowing they could and would take it?"

"I don't care what they take," I said. "Only that they let her live." I locked my desperate eyes on hers. "Alice has to live."

A silence followed. The deepest yet. Not even the fire cracked.

Laughing Crow lowered her head. And when she spoke again, it was softer, almost reverent. "You are not what I expected, Jumilin."

"I've heard that once or twice," I muttered bitterly, straightening up and dusting off my knees.

She chuckled, the sound dry, but not unkind.

"I have walked this land longer than you can imagine," the shaman said. "And I have met many who claimed to love. Claimed to sacrifice. But most of them wanted a bargain that did not leave them bleeding. You..." She shook her head. "You speak as if you've already died. And perhaps that is why the spirits listen."

My throat closed. I didn't know what to say to that. The truth of her words cemented something inside me that I'd refused to acknowledge for a very long time. I did speak like someone that had already died. I lived like it too. I think long before I escaped the cages the first time I knew however this ended it wouldn't be with me standing. And strangely I was okay with that. Dominic shifted behind me as if to remind me I had people to think of now. My ribcage tightened painfully.

Laughing Crow turned her palms upward, cutting my train of thought. "Then let us ask not just for life," she said, "but for mercy."

She drew a blade from her hip, not silver, not iron, but

obsidian. Pure and black as sorrow, a long feather dangling from the hilt.

She cut a line across her palm.

Her blood hit the earth, soaking into it immediately.

"Let her life be spared," she whispered to the wind. "Let the fire that burns her be cooled. Let the voice of her magic be heard and untwisted."

The wind answered.

It did not howl.

It sighed.

The smoke rose again but this time, it moved toward me.

Not like before, not like mist rising from wet earth or incense curling skyward in reverence. No. This smoke had purpose. Sentience. It came like a memory long buried clawing its way back to the surface. It curled around my chest, my arms, my throat, not strangling, not consuming, but weaving through the spaces between bone and breath.

It touched me like an old grief and a forgotten promise. Comforting. Familiar. Alien.

Marking me.

I tried to inhale, but the oxygen was too thick, too heavy with old names and older debts. My lungs burned with the weight of it. My heart thundered a warning, too fast, too loud, but I didn't retreat. I couldn't. The circle held me. The spirits held me. I was theirs now, at least in part.

I couldn't breathe. I couldn't speak. I felt Dominic trashing against the bindings they must've placed on him and my blood curdled in my veins.

And then...

Pain.

Not the blistering kind that tears through flesh or the kind that sears through veins like wildfire. This pain was deeper. Older. A quiet rending from within. Like something long knotted around my soul was finally being unwound, fiber by fiber, strand by strand. Gentle, terrible. A sorrowful release.

As if someone had reached inside and untied a thousand invisible knots that had held me together, and in doing so, showed me how tightly I'd been wound all along.

I gasped. A sound more sob than breath, and collapsed to my knees once again.

The world tilted sideways. The firelight fractured. The circle blurred into nothing but echoes of wind and shadow. My fingers dug into the dirt, clawing at something solid, something real, but even the earth beneath me pulsed like a living thing.

And through the din, through the deafening roar of blood in my ears, Laughing Crow's voice reached me.

Low. Steady. Certain.

"The spirits accept," she said. "But they will take something. They always do."

I nodded, or thought I did. My body no longer felt like mine. My awareness was held together by frayed threads. Gravity no longer obeyed. Time no longer moved. But her voice anchored me.

They will take something.

And I would give it. Whatever they asked, whatever they claimed, I would not resist. I had nothing left to barter except this. This one thing I had never dared to give freely.

Surrender.

The last thing I felt before the dark pulled me under was the spark of magic I had carried my entire life, the legacy of my mother's blood, that quiet ember passed down in silence and shame, beginning to shift.

It didn't go out.

It didn't flare into destruction.

It moved.

Changed.

Not stolen. Not extinguished. Not exiled.

But claimed.

Not entirely mine anymore. Not entirely me.

A new shape.

A new bond.

The magic was now part of something larger, older, deeper than even blood.

And just before consciousness dissolved into starlit shadow, I understood:

It wasn't only my plea the spirits had answered.

It was my belonging they had weighed.

And for now, they had allowed me to stay.

Chapter Twenty

ALICE

It wasn't sleep.

Sleep didn't claw its way through your thoughts, or hum like a thousand wasps caught beneath your skin. It didn't taste like blood and iron, or echo with voices that sounded like your own but spoke in tongues you didn't know.

This was something else. A prison of magic.

I existed in the dark.

There were no walls, but I knew I couldn't run. There was no sky, but I felt like I was falling, perpetually, without end. The curse Frederic had spun through me moved like smoke and barbed wire, curling tight around my mind, burrowing through my memories. I could feel it feeding. It tore through who I had been, distorting the shape of myself in ways I didn't understand.

Sometimes, I would catch glimpses, small flickers, of my own reflection in the black: my eyes too wide, my skin cracked like porcelain, my mouth stitched shut with golden thread. And somewhere far off, like wind brushing through the bones of a ruin, I heard laughter.

His laughter.

But lately… something had shifted.

The darkness still clung, but it didn't fit right anymore. It scratched. It thinned. Like a snake shedding its skin, resisting, then unraveling. The threads of the spell writhed within me, pulling tighter the more I tried to resist.

And I was resisting.

I didn't know how, not truly. But something inside me, a tiny shard, a sliver of defiance maybe, refused to bow. Maybe it had always been there. Maybe it was something I learned from Brooklyn.

Dear Universe, Brooklyn.

The moment I thought her name, pain sliced through me. Not physical but deeper. A truth.

An ache.

She was doing something.

I felt it like a pulse beneath the surface of this nightmare, like a call through water. Something was tearing at the curse from the outside. Gently, but with intent. I could feel her persistence and loyalty to me like a fire being held against glass. Warming. Cracking. Daring me to come back.

Damn, hope was a dangerous thing.

But I knew my friend too well. We were very different but very much alike. If I could feel her as if she stood next to me, then she had to be close to me in a way she shouldn't be. She must have gone to someone. Done something. Promised something. I should know because I would've done the same thing.

My anxiety screamed through the dark. *What did you do?*

The curse hissed at that. It didn't like the intrusion. It didn't like the crack in the wall. The space where light had begun to bleed through.

Suddenly, everything shifted.

It was like being ripped through the fabric of a dream. The sensation wasn't kind or clean. It felt like falling through a mirror, glass shearing through every limb, until…

Heat.

Not flame. Something older. Something alive. It curled around my heart and lungs and bones. It *recognized* me. And more terrifyingly, it recognized Brooklyn.

Something *had* changed. I knew it. Felt it. The curse, once so embedded in me I couldn't tell where it ended and I began, was retreating now. Not destroyed, but folding in on itself like a beast wounded in its den.

The pressure broke. I gasped.

Sound rushed in.

For a long moment, I wasn't sure if I had actually opened my eyes, or if I'd only imagined doing so. Everything was blurry, shifting shapes, half-formed shadows swimming in a haze of amber candlelight and something richer beneath it, like sunlight straining through molasses. I blinked. Once. Twice. The room stilled and focused. Wood-paneled ceiling. Worn rafters. The faint scent of pine and blood and burnt herbs.

I was alive.

"Shit…" Chester's voice cracked mid-word, his hand knocking over a bowl of dried herbs. "Echo, she's…she's looking at me. She's…Holy *shit*, she's awake!"

The blur above me sharpened slightly.

Echo's eyes locked on mine. Her breath caught in her throat. Her hands froze, halfway between my chest and a bowl of glowing sigils etched in salt. Or, sand. Things were very blurry without my glasses. The wolf growled softly near my side, tail low, head tilted. But there was no menace in him. Just stunned reverence.

"Alice?" Echo whispered, voice trembling, as if she was afraid saying my name might shatter the moment.

My mouth was dry. My lips cracked. But I forced the word past them anyway.

"Hey. This is not actually hell, right? I mean I'm awake in my own world? Right?"

Chester whooped so loud I flinched. "Oh, dear *gods*, she's actually talking. She's *alive!*"

He grabbed Echo in a wild embrace, spinning her around despite her protests.

"I'm fine," I rasped, even though it was a bald-faced lie. Every nerve in my body was fried. My skin felt like it was made of bruises and regret. But I was awake.

Alive.

Lucid.

I blinked again, the weight of the room settling in around me. I was back in the safe house. The cot beneath me was firm and familiar, and someone had clearly tried to make me comfortable, too many blankets, too many cushions, but all of it with *care*. There were runes drawn on the walls. Burnt candles on every available surface. The smell of incense, medicinal herbs, and desperation lingered thick in the air.

The wolf was still beside me, eyes locked onto mine like he didn't trust the world not to take me again. His fur was still matted with blood. Mine? Someone else's? I didn't care. His presence made my chest ache with gratitude.

But one presence was missing.

"Where's Brooklyn?" I asked, heart stammering.

Chester froze. Echo hesitated, eyeing me like one would eye a snake debating if it would slither away or bite you.

"She's not hurt," Echo said finally. "She's not…hurt. She's okay. She just… went to get help."

"That's vague," I muttered. "even for a demon."

"She went to the reservation," she clarified after a beat. "To the shaman. Laughing Crow."

My blood turned to ice. "She... *what*?"

"You didn't give us a choice, Alice," Echo muttered, almost put out as if I was trying to be difficult just to make her day miserable. "You were barely breathing. Rowan's still barely alive. Samir won't speak to any of us—he is hiding in his room. She said she'd *do anything* to get help. She left hours ago. Dominic went with her."

My breath caught in my chest. I didn't need to ask what Brooklyn meant by *anything*. I could feel it in the pit of my stomach, the way the spell inside me had changed. Rewritten itself. Not vanished, no. But no longer trying to consume me. Someone had paid its toll.

And that someone had been her.

"No, no, no," I mumbled, trying to sit up. "We have to go. We have to stop her, get her to undo whatever stupid..."

"You're not going anywhere," Echo snapped, her touch gentler than her words. She pushed me back down with a surprisingly steady hand. "You're *barely* here as it is. You just clawed your way back from whatever spell that bastard laid into your veins. Sit. Breathe. Let your body remember how to be whole again. The last thing I need is for Brooklyn to kill me because I let you get out of bed." She muttered that last part under her breath.

"But she..."

"She's Brooklyn," Echo said simply. "And that means she's strong. And also, the most reckless, bull-headed creature I've ever met until she introduced me to you. If there's a fight to be had for your life, she's not losing it."

Chester stepped forward, his grin softer now. "She told Dominic she'd wait. No violence. No threats. Just words."

I swallowed hard. "That's not her way." I eyed him although he was very blurry, like he had grown a second head. "We are talking about Brooklyn, right? You've met the girl."

"That should tell you how bad you were if she was willing to put blades and fangs aside just to get help," he said.

I lay back against the pillows, trembling, my muscles aching with exhaustion. I could feel the remnants of the spell like soot in my lungs, but I could also feel *her*. Brooklyn. Not just a memory or a name but something warm threaded through the wreckage of me. Like a bond lit from within.

She'd bargained with the shaman; I knew it as well as I knew my name. I didn't know what the price was that she had to pay, but I knew it would never be light.

I closed my eyes, letting tears fall freely now. Not because I was weak. But because I was *alive*. And because she had to sacrifice something to bring me back to the world of the living. I was tired of being a burden, a liability to her. Despite all my shortcomings, there she went again.

She'd saved me.

Again.

And when she returned, gods help whoever tried to stop me from saving *her* right back. I was going to pluck Laughing Crow's hair one by one until she undid whatever she did to my friend.

After that I was going to sleep.

And eat something.

Not necessarily in that order.

Chapter Twenty-One

BROOKLYN

Every muscle in my body trembled so violently, I half expected to rattle apart. Twitching, aching, burning with the weight of what I had just given, what had been taken, my limbs jerked in uncontrollable spasms. You'd think I'd sprinted across the continent in a single day. And honestly, even for someone like me, supernatural or not, that would be a feat beyond comprehension.

And yet there I was, shivering like a fevered leaf in the eye of a storm.

Dominic held me as if I were made of glass and sacred fire. His arms, iron-wrapped velvet. His heartbeat, steady, strong, unyielding, thundered against my ribs like a war drum laced with comfort. Ever the calm inside my chaos, my mate stood like a sentry between me and the consequences of my bargain. A wall of devotion in the aftermath of what I'd unleashed.

He hadn't waited. Not for permission, not for protocol, not for sense. The moment the protective barrier of the ritual circle had flickered out, he was there. Storming forward like a predator denied its mate for too long, scooping me into his arms without a second glance toward the others.

Laughing Crow had protested. Loudly. Unapologetically. She had barked some demand about leaving the circle intact for spiritual equilibrium or residual reading. I couldn't track the exact words through the fog in my head, but Dominic was deaf to it. His snarl at the shaman had rattled through my chest like the growl of thunder rolling in after lightning. I felt it more than heard it.

He cradled me close, pressing his lips to my temple, breathing me in like he was reassuring himself I was still here, still breathing.

I was, but only barely.

I could feel something inside me unspooling still, slow and irreversible. Not breaking. Not burning. But… shifting. Re-aligning into something new.

And I didn't want to speak of it. Not yet. Maybe not ever.

"She needs to rest," the shaman snapped from somewhere near my shoulder. "There are still variables in motion. You'll stay. I must monitor her for anomalies in her energy, her mind. What she opened tonight wasn't clean magic. The spirits always take their due."

"Get away from her, you deranged human," Dominic growled, and I winced at the rawness in his tone. I could feel the fury coursing through him like a storm with no place to land. "You've done enough."

I wanted to hush him, to soothe the ache behind his eyes, but I didn't have the strength. Not when each breath still carried echoes of fire and bone-deep fatigue. So instead, I buried my face in the curve of his neck, the scent of him grounding me, filling my nostrils with cedar smoke, heat, and the faintest trace of blood still clinging to him after our ordeal at the cages.

Laughing Crow, to her credit, didn't flinch at his tone. Didn't cower before the beast he held barely in check.

"If she hadn't come to me," she countered coolly, "your precious Alice would be dead. You think you could've undone that curse on your own, *cat*?"

Her smirk was infuriating.

Dominic's chest rumbled beneath me. "Our Alice," he corrected, biting off each word. "Don't you mean *your* Alice too? She carries blood from your people, does she not? Or do you reserve your loyalty for only the convenient children of your bloodline?"

There was a pause. Heavy. Laced with an unspeakable something.

It was like time itself hesitated, uncertain if it should keep moving.

And then I saw it.

A flicker in the shaman's eyes. Subtle. Fleeting. But undeniable.

Shock.

She masked it quickly, too quickly, but the damage had been done.

I lifted my head from Dominic's chest, the weight of his words settling over me like a mantle of cold iron. "What did you just say?" I rasped, voice dry and rough like wind scraping over salt.

"She has roots here," Dominic murmured, his voice low and rough, cutting through the air with sharp clarity. He didn't look at me, didn't need to. His words weren't for me alone. "Did you not wonder why her soul burns so loudly in this land that even I could feel it from outside the circle? Why the spirits stirred like wind through dry leaves at the sound of her pain?" He paused, his nose twitching faintly. "I can smell it, too. They carry the same note…your wolves, your trees, your wards. She has it. It's in her blood. The same scent Alice carries."

The air thickened like a held breath.

My heart stuttered.

I turned to Laughing Crow slowly, dread pooling behind my ribs. Her gaze, always so penetrating, so direct, was now cast aside. She wouldn't meet my eyes.

"I thought…" My voice splintered mid-sentence. I swallowed hard, pushing through the tremor that curled in my throat. "I thought it was just a mistake. I could smell her when we stepped onto the reservation, but I chalked it up to being able to find her anywhere. I thought I was imagining things because I was worried sick about her."

Still, silence.

A silence too full to be empty.

Dominic's arms tightened around me, pulling me closer, as if bracing me for a truth he already understood. "You made no mistake," he said firmly, each word striking like a war drum. "And this woman damn well knows it."

At last, Laughing Crow looked at me.

Not with the sharp eyes of a sentinel. Not with the cold detachment of a shaman measuring weight and worth. But with something heavier, something that lived deep in the marrow and did not age with years.

"I did not know," she said quietly. "Not with certainty. But when I looked at her for the first time, I felt the land murmur. It does not speak often. But it remembered her blood."

My chest tightened as if bound by cords of memory I never wove. "Then you should've said something," I whispered. "You should've told me."

"So, you just let her nearly die anyway?" Dominic's voice was all claws and thunder now. "You heard the land call her home, and still you left my mate burning on your floor. You let Brooklyn bargain for a life that should've been protected here."

Laughing Crow didn't flinch. "She offered her life freely. And I do not interfere with the sacred will of the spirits. Alice's blood may call to the land, but her choices, her fury, her grief, her guilt…They belong solely to her. I do not stand between a soul and the storm it summons."

"That's convenient," Dominic bit out. "You're very good at telling yourself stories to justify letting people suffer."

The shaman's dark gaze flashed. "You think I don't carry ghosts of my own, *cat*? You think I don't know the price of interference? This land has bled under our care. Bled for our mistakes. Ancient magic demands balance, and you expect me to tip the scales without consequence?"

"I expect you to honor blood," Dominic snapped.

Silence pulsed through the room, sharp as shattered bone.

I slowly pulled away from him and sat up straighter, letting my feet touch the ground. The ache that rippled through me was deep, not physical. It was older than flesh. I met Laughing Crow's eyes without flinching.

"You say the land remembers her," I said, voice steadier now, carved from something brittle but unyielding. "Then what is she? What is it remembering?"

She watched me for a long time, unreadable. Then, in a softer voice, as if speaking not to me, but to the space between us, she said, "The Great Spirit does not speak about Alice, child." I almost laughed that she called me a child when I was probably older than her by hundreds of years. "It speaks about you." Something other shifted in her pitch-black eyes and I started rethinking my certainty of who was older than whom.

"Me?" Shock evident on my face and in my tone, I reached for Dominic's hand instinctively knowing that this human was about to pull the ground from under my feet.

"You are a child of two forgotten truths. One born of fire, one born of earth. The land remembers your mother's sorrow. The blood that fled and never came home. You were not supposed to step foot on our land. And yet... here you are walking our soil as if you were born to do so. Asking to die for someone else. And the land answered not because of who you are now... but because of who you were always meant to be."

My breath caught, ragged and unformed.

I didn't understand all of it. But I knew this: something ancient and hidden inside me was being unearthed. Slowly. Irrevocably confirming the truth in her words.

Dominic tightened his hold on my fingers. I gripped his without looking away from her.

"Then help me dig through those forgotten truths, Shaman," I said. "I'll walk into every fire and sift every ash if I have to. But I'm done letting people speak for me or use me for their gain. If the land remembers me, then maybe it's time I remember it, as well."

Laughing Crow inclined her head, just barely. But the glint in her dark eyes had changed. Wariness had not vanished. But something else settled in behind it.

Respect.

"We'll speak again soon," she said. "When you're ready. Not before."

Then she turned, her shawl sweeping the floor like

trailing feathers, and headed toward the trees, the scent of sage and the echo of ancestral breath trailing behind her.

"You said the spirits took something," I called out to her. "And I felt it. I need to know... what changed."

Laughing Crow looked back over her shoulder. "You are not dying. That's what matters."

"That's not what I asked."

She studied me, then turned around slowly tilting her head, as if listening to something far off.

"The magic in your blood is no longer bound, girl. It's... layered now. Altered. Intertwined with something older. The cost was not your life, but the shape of your gift. It belongs to more than just you now. The Fates waited for a chance to alter your destiny. You opened that door for them tonight."

Dominic's voice was ice. "Stop speaking in riddles, human, or I will break your neck. What does that mean?"

Laughing Crow's black eyes flicked between us. "It means the spirits did not take her power. They made it *free*. We will all see what that means in time. I am the Great Spirit servant, I am not a seer to see the future."

Silence fell again when Laughing Crow turned her back to us and walked away, but this one felt different.

Not tense.

Final.

Dominic carried me back to the house to a woven mat near the hearth and laid me down carefully, his arms still wrapped around my waist as if letting go might invite some invisible hand to take me from him.

I didn't fight it.

After a long moment he settled next to me and pulled me gently into his arms once more. "Are you all right?"

"No," I said truthfully, burying my face into the safety of

his chest. "But I think I'm finally on the edge of some real answers."

He held me there for a long time.

And for once, neither of us filled the silence. We just let the land breathe. Let the house watch. Let the truth settle like dust between bones once forgotten, now stirring again.

For the first time in hours, maybe days, the trembling had stopped.

But nothing felt settled.

Not yet.

Because whatever shifted inside me...

Was just beginning to wake.

Chapter Twenty-Two

DOMINIC

Something had to change.

Long-lived or not, I had a feeling my heart would give out if my mate continued to throw herself at danger at every turn.

She thrashed all night, fighting unseen monsters from her psyche that I could not tear apart or shred with my bare hands. So, I watched her now from where I stood near the threshold of the shaman's house barely lit by the coals still smoldering in the fire-burning stove, her silhouette hunched, fingers pressed to her temples like the weight of the world still hadn't finished grinding her down. Her breathing was shallow but even. Her spirit, though, it was unraveling. Just in silence now, instead of screams and whimpers.

She'd given too much. Again.

And like a fool, I let her.

The guilt crawled down my spine like something alive; Feral and unrelenting, its claws sinking into every vertebra with merciless precision. I had sworn, sworn with every breath in my body, that I would never again stand idly by while she bled for the people she loved. And yet, I had done just that. I had watched as she stepped willingly into a circle etched with power older than the bones of the earth, and offered herself, body, soul, and magic, to spirits that existed long before time itself.

I didn't stop her.

I couldn't.

Because somewhere deep beneath my skin, in the place where instinct and reason warred, I understood: had I tried to interfere, she wouldn't have hesitated to fight me. Not with claws or fangs, but with the sheer fire of her will. And it wasn't the pain of her fury I feared. It was the fracture it would leave between us. Her rage would not cut me down, but it would cast me out. And in that moment, nothing was more important to her than the war she chose to fight. Not the Syndicate. Not her own survival.

Saving Alice.

That was her holy ground. Her line in the sand. And I... I was just trying not to lose the only thing in this world still tethering me to something good.

Still, the question pulsed beneath every beat of my heart. How long could we survive like this? How many more sacrifices before there was nothing left of her to save?

The door creaked behind me. Laughing Crow's light tread brushed the wooden floor as she entered. She didn't speak. Not at first. Just stood beside me in the shadows and stared at Brooklyn the same way one watches the sea after a storm: searching for what it left behind, and what it took.

"She's stubborn," I said, not looking at the shaman. "I wish she wasn't." I muttered to myself.

Laughing Crow didn't move. "She's fire walking on bone."

"Is that your poetic way of telling me she's breaking?"

"No." The shaman finally folded her arms. "It means she's dangerous. To herself. To others. But mostly to the things that would try to take her light. She says she doesn't care what she pays but she will defy the universe to keep her light intact."

I let out a humorless breath. "Tell me something I don't know."

"You fear she'll die," the old woman said simply, still not looking at me.

I didn't answer. What was I supposed to say to that? Lie?

She turned her head slightly, studying me now. "You carry the weight of a protector. But what happens when the threat isn't from outside?"

My jaw clenched. "Then I protect her from herself. Even if she hates me for it."

A quiet hum of approval. "Then you're not as blind as I thought."

I looked at her now, finally, forcing my hands to curl into fists so I didn't grab her by the throat. "Did the spirits take something from her? Tell me the truth."

Laughing Crow's expression gave nothing away. "They always take something. But not always in the way you expect."

"That's not an answer."

She gave me a small, sharp smile. "And yet, it's the truth."

I turned away before I did something reckless, like kill her, or drag her into another circle and demand clarity. The only clarity I needed was in Brooklyn's pulse, in the way her eyes stayed open now, not clouded by pain.

She was alive.

But for how long?

I crossed the floor and crouched beside her. She didn't look up, but she didn't pull away either. Her energy pulsed erratically through the bond, flickering between numbness and the low throb of something unresolved.

I reached for her hand, threading our fingers together.

"I can't lose you," I said softly. "And you can't keep throwing yourself into the fire expecting me to drag you back every time without it killing me first. One day there won't be anything left to pull free, Brooklyn. What will become of me then?"

Her breath hitched. Just barely.

I leaned in, my voice lower. "You don't have to do this alone. You never did."

"I know," she whispered. "But I didn't know how to let anyone else carry the burden of my kind's sins."

"You don't have to allow me to carry it for you," I murmured. "You just have to let me carry you with it."

She finally looked at me, eyes rimmed with exhaustion but clearer than before. "I don't know how to stop fighting, Dominic."

"Then don't," I said, brushing her cheek with my thumb. "Just don't fight alone. That is all I ask. Let me fight whatever it is with you, next to you."

And for the first time in a long while, she didn't argue.

The fire crackled low beside us, casting lazy shadows that danced against the far wall. The smell of herbs, sage, pine, the acrid bite of valerian, clung to the beams and to my skin. But beyond the scents, beyond the shimmer of soft embers, the land outside pressed in. Silent. Waiting.

She leaned her head against my shoulder and exhaled like the weight of all her choices might finally tip her sideways. I didn't move. Didn't speak. Just let her be exactly where she needed to be, alive, breathing, and within arm's reach.

A shudder went through her then. Not cold, but like a memory come to life. I recognized it for what it was: the aftermath of giving too much.

"I felt something shift," she murmured. "When the spirits answered. I thought it would take me with it. I thought I wouldn't come back."

I closed my eyes and swallowed. "Then next time when we need help, we find a way that doesn't require blood. No more sacrifices, for either of us."

She didn't answer. Her fingers tightened around mine instead.

"I need you whole," I said, my voice a quiet rasp against the hush of the room. "Not just because I'm your mate. Not just because I love. But because they'll come for you again. For all of us. And if you keep giving away pieces of yourself every time one of us is hurt…" I swallowed, hard. "You'll disappear before we ever make it to the end. You'll bleed out in spirit long before they get the chance to kill you."

She didn't argue. She didn't even flinch. Instead, her head shifted slightly against my chest, her fingers curling unconsciously into the folds of my shirt like she was holding onto the only thing in the world still tethering her here. I felt her breath move in small, shallow currents, each inhale threading through my ribs like a prayer she wasn't sure she still had the right to speak.

Her voice, when it came, was barely audible. "But I didn't push you away this time." A pause. "At least not when it mattered."

My throat tightened. "No," I agreed, the word heavy in my mouth. "You didn't."

And it had meant everything. That she let me stay. That she hadn't turned me into an enemy simply because I wouldn't stand by and watch her die. That she had finally, finally trusted me enough to remain at her side while the earth itself weighed her soul in its hand.

She shifted again, and I looked down as she tilted her head back to meet my gaze. There was something in her eyes, something broken, yes, but still fiercely alive. Still burning. A kind of quiet, exhausted defiance that made my chest ache with a longing I didn't have words for. She'd walked through hell again for someone else, and still came back with her spine unbent.

"Promise me something," she said.

My breath caught. "Anything."

As soon as the words were out of my mouth I regretted them. I would not, and could not promise her anything. Not when it came to her safety and life. I stayed silent though like the coward I was.

"If it comes down to it…" Her voice faltered, just for a beat. "And I have to make that choice again…you won't stop me."

The words lanced through me like a blade to the gut. Cold, clean, and impossibly sharp. My first instinct was to tell her no. To swear I would chain her down with my own body before I'd let her burn herself to ash again. But I didn't lie to her. I never would.

My jaw clenched, and it took every ounce of control I had to steady my voice. "I'll try," I said, the words scraping raw against my throat. "But don't ask me to let you die. Not without tearing the world apart first."

She stared at me for a long, quiet moment, eyes darker than night, shimmering faintly in the glow from the burning stove. Then, slowly, something softened in her expression, some hard edge easing back just enough to let the humanity bleed through.

She smiled. Faint. Crooked. A curve of pain and gratitude both.

And this time, she leaned her forehead against mine.

"If it comes down to it," she whispered, "we'll tear it apart together, then."

And I knew deep down to the marrow of my bones that she meant it.

She wasn't bluffing. She never had been. If the world demanded her blood again, she'd bleed for it. But this time, she wouldn't do it alone. Not if I had breath left in my body. We would tear through the veil of fate itself. Rip down the heavens and unmake every damn law written in fire and bone if that's what it took.

Even if it killed us.

And in the sacred quiet that followed, I held her closer, felt the uneven rhythm of her heartbeat sync slowly with mine. I let the silence settle not like a burden, but like a vow. One I intended to keep no matter what came next.

Because we weren't done yet.

And gods help anyone who thought they could take her from me again.

Chapter Twenty-Three

BROOKLYN

In slow, deliberate waves, I became aware of Dominic's body pressed to mine—solid, grounding, real. His breath ghosted over my lips with each exhale, warm and steady, a lifeline in the lingering dark. It was as if the world had narrowed to just this: the cadence of his breathing, the faint thrum of his heartbeat against my chest, the way his presence filled the space around me with silent, unyielding devotion.

My body, aching and frayed at the edges, pushed away everything else, the lingering pain, the dizzying exhaustion, even the roiling uncertainty. All of it receded, eclipsed by the gravity of him. Every nerve in me, every flicker of awareness, redirected toward him with single-minded clarity, like a compass needle finding true north.

He didn't speak. He didn't have to.

My soul knew his voice even in silence. And my body answered his nearness not with fear or hesitation but with aching familiarity. A recognition deeper than blood or bond.

In the hush that followed, I remained still. Wrapped in the quiet gravity of him. My forehead rested lightly against his, the smallest space between us charged with heat, with tension, with something far older than the bond that tied us. This wasn't desire born from adrenaline or circumstance. This was the deep, aching need of one soul recognizing its other half and daring, finally, to reach for it.

His hand slid slowly up my back, the calluses on his palm catching the fabric of my shirt as if even his fingers didn't trust this moment to last. He held me like I might dissolve in his arms. Like if he let go, I would slip back into the darkness and never return.

"You're still trembling," he murmured against my cheek, his voice rough, velveted with concern.

"Not from fear," I whispered. "Not anymore."

His fingers stilled. Then curled tighter.

I tilted my head just enough that our mouths hovered in the same breath, close, but not touching. A held note waiting to resolve. My lips were parted, breath shallow, the ache of anticipation shimmering just beneath my skin. I could feel the pulse in his neck. Could feel how tightly he held himself still.

And that restraint... it undid me.

Because I knew how hard it was for him. To want and not take. To burn and not consume.

"You can touch me," I said, the words barely more than breath. "I'm here. I'm not breaking."

His hand came to my jaw slowly, reverently. His thumb traced the curve of my cheekbone like it was sacred, like *I* was sacred. That reverence was the most devastating thing about him. Dominic had teeth. He had claws. He had a past bathed in blood and fury. But when he touched me... it was always like this. As if I were the last star in his sky and he had only one lifetime left to worship me.

He kissed me then. Not hard, not urgent, but deep. Slow. Anchoring.

His mouth moved over mine like a vow. No promises spoken, yet each brush of his lips said everything: I'm here. I see you. I won't let go.

I melted into him, my hands fisting in the fabric of his shirt, dragging him closer until nothing remained between us but skin and breath and the heat building like a storm about to break. The taste of him, warm, earthy, wild, slid over my tongue and I moaned quietly into the kiss, a sound that made him shudder.

Dominic responded with a low growl, the sound vibrating against my mouth as his other hand found my waist, pulling me fully into his lap. The pressure of his body against mine lit something deeper, more primal, a hunger coiled in my belly I hadn't let myself feel in too long.

Still, he didn't rush. His touch never lost that reverence.

Fingers glided up my ribs, over my back, mapping every inch of me with maddening patience, learning me all over again. His kisses traveled to my jaw, to my throat, leaving fire in their wake. My head tilted to give him more space, and he took it, his mouth finding the sensitive hollow below my ear and making me gasp.

The air thickened, the room forgotten, and even time itself stood suspended.

He drew back just enough to look at me, his eyes almost black, the green swallowed by his pupils with want, but beneath it... fear. Not of me. But the fear of hurting me. Of pushing too far, too soon.

"You sure?" he asked, his voice barely holding together. "I can stop. Say the word and I will."

Gods, I loved him for that.

And it made me want him even more.

I cupped his face in both hands, thumbs grazing the stubble along his jaw. "I'm not made of glass, Dominic. I *want* this. I want *you*."

A flicker of relief. A flare of something deeper.

His breath still ghosted over my lips, warm and steady, each exhale a tether holding me to the present. The storm inside me, the grief, the rage, the fear, began to unravel thread by thread, tugged loose by the gentle weight of his touch. Every part of me that had curled into a defensive ball softened against him now. Not because I was suddenly safe. Not because the danger had passed.

But because he was here. And that was all that mattered. That was enough.

Dominic didn't move, not at first. He simply watched me with eyes that had seen too much violence, too much loss, and yet still held a reverence for softness, especially mine. When his fingers brushed a lock of hair from my temple, the fire red strand sliding tenderly between his fingers, I felt my whole-body sigh beneath his touch. I hadn't even known I was holding my breath until that very moment.

"I thought I lost you today," he murmured, voice rough with everything he hadn't said.

I closed my eyes, pressing my cheek against his palm. "I think I almost lost myself."

"Don't say that." His thumb swept gently along my jaw. "You're still here. Still *you*. Even when the world tries to take pieces."

I opened my eyes to meet his, the ache in my chest blooming into something warmer, heavier. "That's only true because you're here to remind me of what I have to lose."

He leaned in then, slow and certain, giving me time to stop him but I didn't want him to stop. His lips met mine, not with urgency, but with barely contained passion. A kiss meant not to claim, but to ask. To assure.

Every other time we had come so close to death or unknown terrors loomed over our heads that our love-making was always hot, explosive, a single-minded purpose of claiming as if that would remind us we were still alive. This time he was taking his time. That was telling how strong the fear of losing me was inside him. This time he was reassuring himself I am still here.

And I answered with the same gentleness, with the same quiet hunger.

His hand slid to the small of my back, drawing me closer. The heat of his body seeped into mine like sunlight through a storm. When our foreheads touched again, our breathing found a shared rhythm. One heartbeat, split between two bodies. I felt the quiet restraint in him, the tension barely leashed beneath his skin, like he was holding back a wildfire out of respect for the scorched earth I had become.

But I didn't want restraint.

I wanted him.

"Touch me," I whispered, the words caught on a breath I couldn't quite release.

His hands trembled slightly as they obeyed, one splaying across the curve of my back, the other cupping the side of my neck. He kissed me again, deeper this time, a groan slipping from his throat and humming into mine. The sound pulled something low and desperate from my core.

Dominic kissed like someone who worshipped storms. Like someone who knew what it meant to survive them.

And I kissed back like someone trying to find home.

We didn't speak after that. Words became obsolete. The brush of skin against skin, the slide of breath between parted mouths, the way our bodies curved instinctively to meet one another. *That* was the language now.

His jacket fell from his shoulders first, landing with a soft thud on the floor. My fingertips chased the warmth of his skin beneath his shirt, marveling at how alive he felt. How alive *I* felt. Every sigh he gave sent a tremor down my spine. Every quiet gasp, every low growl deep in his chest, etched itself into my bones.

And I clung to him, not like holding a lifeline, but like something fierce, like someone who had already walked through fire and wasn't afraid to burn again, as long as it was with him.

He kissed down the line of my throat, slow and reverent, his breath feathering across the sensitive skin as he murmured my name like a promise. My hands threaded through his hair, desperate to anchor myself in the moment before it slipped away and became nothing.

"Brooklyn," he said, the syllables a graveled prayer.

"You have me. I'm here," I whispered. "Still here."

He made love to me slowly, reverently. Every shift of his hips pushing him deeper and forcing my channel to clench from the fullness. Every brush of his lips left scorched skin in their wake. My oversensitive skin was ready to combust and pressure started coiling like a too tight spring in my lower belly. Our movements became erratic, the touch more frantic as we chased the promise of ecstasy together until I was pushed over the edge on a gasp that was more a moan and he followed me through it.

"Still here." I rasped in his ear when I caught my breath.

And for that moment while wrapped in his arms, our

bodies connected impossibly close that you couldn't tell where he ended and I began, drowning in the steady beat of his heart against mine, I believed it.

Chapter Twenty-Four

DOMINIC

I couldn't believe our luck when we finally convinced the shaman that Brooklyn was well enough to travel back to the house. The trees parted around us like old sentinels, letting us pass without fanfare or farewell as if they too couldn't wait for us to be out of that place. The path away from the reservation was narrow and overgrown, dappled in soft shafts of morning light that pierced the canopy above. Each step we took away from Laughing Crow's home felt heavier than it should have. Not because of exhaustion, though gods knew we were both bone-deep tired, but because of what waited for us on the other side.

Or what might not wait for us.

A lump formed in my throat the size of a fist.

Brooklyn walked just ahead of me, silent, her posture rigid with frustration she didn't bother hiding. The wind caught her hair now and again, lifting it like strands of dark flame. She hadn't said a word since we passed the last set of wards.

I watched her shoulders rise and fall with each breath,

the tension in her muscles as tight as a drawn bow. Her silence wasn't the kind that invited comfort. It was the kind built from self-blame, from fire that couldn't be cooled with logic. She carried her guilt like armor, welded to her bones.

"You're thinking about Rowan," I said gently, catching up to her side.

"I'm thinking about all of them," she answered without looking at me. "But yes. Mostly Rowan."

Her voice was low, bitter with guilt. I could feel the weight of it in her words, like ash clinging to the back of my throat.

"I know it's not rational," she continued, finally glancing my way. "But I can't help feeling like we should've done more. Pressed harder. Forced the shaman to say more than just that cryptic bullshit."

"She didn't lie to you," I said carefully. "She said you'd know when the time was right. That's not the kind of thing you can drag out of someone before it's ready."

Brooklyn stopped walking. Her boots crushed a patch of moss beneath her, and her fists clenched at her sides. "I know Alice is awake and recovering. And don't ask me how I know that, it's freaky enough as it is to feel the certainty without trying to explain it. But Rowen? He's still unconscious, Dominic. Every hour we spend away from him…"

"Is another hour he's still breathing," I said quietly.

She exhaled harshly through her nose, jaw tight with unspoken anguish. There was no salve for this kind of hurt. No spell or charm to soothe the gnawing doubt in her heart.

Her jaw twitched, but she didn't argue. Just turned her face back to the trees, like the bark might offer some wisdom we hadn't found yet.

"I know you want more answers," I went on. "Hell, so

do I. But we're not going back empty-handed. Alice is alive. The curse is broken. That matters."

"But what if I traded one life for another?" she whispered. "What if saving her means Rowan doesn't wake up?" She faltered for a second then on a heavy sigh rubbed a hand over her face. "And I could never feel guilty for saving Alice over someone else. Which makes me a shitty person."

I stepped closer, placing a hand on her shoulder. She let me, though her body was tense beneath my palm.

"You didn't trade anything," I said. "The spirits took what they wanted. They would've taken it whether you begged or not."

"I just… I can't help thinking she knew. Laughing Crow. She knew Rowan needed something. But she wouldn't say what."

"She didn't say it," I agreed. "But maybe she didn't have to. Maybe it's not her place. Maybe it's yours."

That made her pause.

The trees creaked around us, as if leaning in to listen. Somewhere far behind, a bird called. A lonesome note that faded too quickly. I watched her blink against the light filtering through the leaves, as if trying to push away her thoughts, but they stuck to her like burrs.

"I don't know how to save him," she admitted, and the cracks in her voice nearly undid me.

"You don't have to yet," I said. "Not today. Today we go back. We gather our people. We heal what we can. The rest… we'll face it together." Taking her hand, I pulled her to a stop so she had to look at me. "You'll be able to think better after you see with your own eyes that Alice is on the mend. Yes? And then the three of us will figure out how to help Rowen together."

For a moment, she was still. The forest quieted with her as if listening.

And then she nodded. "Together," she echoed. "I think you are right. I do need to see she's okay with my own eyes before I stop panicking internally."

We started walking again, this time with less silence between us. The wind picked up behind us like a sigh, and I felt, if only faintly, the shift in the world. Something waiting.

Whatever it was, we'd face it side by side.

Still, I couldn't shake the unease tightening my gut. The same sense I'd had in the mansion, the feeling that something had touched us and left its mark. A presence that hadn't shown its full face yet. It clung to my skin like shadow. Maybe it was Rowan's lingering magic, or something worse. I didn't know. But I knew better than to ignore it.

Brooklyn noticed my pause and looked over her shoulder, the early sun outlining her like firelight. "What is it?"

"Nothing," I said automatically, then corrected myself. "Just... keep your guard up when we get there. I don't think our troubles stayed behind."

She gave me a tired smile, one that didn't quite reach her eyes. "They never do."

We walked the rest of the way to the waiting car with weapons sheathed but ready, hearts heavier than any sword.

The gravel crunched beneath our boots in a rhythm that should have been comforting, steady, familiar, but instead echoed like a countdown. Each step toward the vehicle felt like an inch deeper into something unknown. Brooklyn said nothing more, and I didn't push her. We both knew the moment we opened that car door, the world would be waiting to bleed us again.

The reservation faded behind us with each step, the

trees thinning, the powerful, watchful hum of the land giving way to the brittle tension of the human world. But the magic lingered. In our bones. In the silence between us. In the bruised sky above, just starting to flush with the heat of early sun.

The car was right where we'd left it, dust-swept and quiet, as if it had been holding its breath for our return. I opened the door for her, fingers curling once on the handle before I forced myself to let go of the hesitation clawing at me.

Brooklyn paused just before slipping into the passenger seat. Her hand hovered at the doorframe, her jaw tight with unspoken truths. She wasn't just worried. We were past worry. She was preparing. Bracing. For grief. For questions. For the possibility that the time we'd spent away had cost us more than we could afford.

She glanced up at me. "This feeling… What if Alice is not awake…"

"Then we do what needs to be done," I said softly, finishing the thought she didn't want to voice. "One step at a time. If she's not awake we go find Frederic and force him to help her."

Her throat bobbed as she swallowed hard. Then she nodded and slid into the seat, her silence more eloquent than anything words could've offered.

I got behind the wheel, started the engine, and let the low rumble fill the void between us.

We didn't speak for miles.

But the silence wasn't empty.

Brooklyn's fingers fidgeted in her lap, the only sign of the storm beneath her skin. I didn't blame her for it. I felt it too. That unsettled edge like something was waiting for us, crouched in the shadows of the future, teeth bared. The kind of tension you couldn't place until it pounced.

At one point, I glanced over at her.

She was staring out the window, but not really seeing anything. Her mind was elsewhere, probably curled up in the safe house hallway, trying to will Rowan's chest to rise. Her knuckles were white against her thighs.

"I hate this part," she murmured eventually.

"What part?"

"The not-knowing. It's like being halfway through a nightmare, trying to decide if you'll wake up or sink further into it."

I reached over and laced my fingers through hers. "Whatever's waiting…good or bad…we face it together."

She squeezed my hand once before letting go, then exhaled. "I know. I just… I'm scared it won't be enough."

I didn't say it, but I was scared too. Not of the fight. Never that. But of what it would cost her. What more the world might ask from someone who had already given so much.

The sun climbed slowly behind us, gilding the tips of the pines in pale gold. The kind of light that should've meant hope. But to me, it felt more like the quiet before the next scream.

When we finally turned down the familiar dirt road toward the safe house, the knot in my gut pulled tighter. The house came into view slowly, too slowly. And still, nothing moved.

No sign of Echo.

No sign of Chester.

No sign of the wolf.

Brooklyn sat up straighter, hands braced on the dashboard. Her breath hitched.

I slowed the car, every muscle in my body coiled like wire.

We exited the car silently and started for the door but Brooklyn stopped and picked up something from the long steps leading to the front patio. When I reached her, I found her holding Alice's glasses, turning them between her fingers before she glanced at me.

"Why would she leave her glasses here?" a line deepened between her brows.

"Maybe she was sitting here waiting for you and forgot that she left them on the steps?" It sounded dumb even to my own ears. Alice couldn't see enough to walk without them, why would she leave them behind?

The expression on Brooklyn's face said she was thinking the same, but she didn't want to voice it. "Yeah, maybe she was waiting," she muttered instead and moved toward the front door with purpose. We both knew one thing for sure.

Something was waiting in that house.

I just prayed if it was something bad, that it was something I could kill.

That would make my day for sure.

Chapter Twenty-Five

BROOKLYN

The door creaked open like it resented us returning.

My hand hovered over the doorknob, fighting a weird feeling that the ground under my feet was shifting. But that can't be a bad omen, can it? We were long overdue for some good news, for something nice to befall us.

The house was quiet, you could say a bit too quiet. Not the kind of silence that followed sleep or stillness, but the brittle hush that wrapped around guilt and grief. I stepped inside slowly, clutching Alice's glasses like a lifeline, the weight of the last twenty-four hours still clinging to my bones. My boots scuffed the floor with every step, and behind me, Dominic's presence followed like a second spine, rigid, watchful, wound tight with the same unease thrumming through me.

The scent of rosemary and faint blood hung in the air. Not fresh. Faded. Echo's attempts at warding, probably. Or maybe her attempt at helping Alice.

Dear gods, Alice.

My steps quickened. I was halfway to the stairs before movement caught my eye. A shadow detaching from the hallway near the living room. Slow. Hesitant.

Samir.

He was standing partially in the dark, hair a disheveled mess, eyes shadowed and bloodshot. His clothes were wrinkled, his posture a far cry from the confident arrogance he usually wore like a second skin. He looked like something that had been gnawed on from the inside out.

"Planning to keep sulking in the hallway until the house burns down around you?" I asked, voice cold as steel, the annoyance from his stupid behavior drilling a hole in my brain.

He flinched. Actually flinched.

"You're back," he said, like he wasn't sure if it was real. "Alice...she's awake."

"No thanks to you, she's not."

The air turned sharp. Behind me, I could feel Dominic's energy shift. He sharply focused on Samir, on alert, coiled tight, already reading the room with deadly precision.

Samir's mouth opened, then closed again. I stepped forward.

"Speak," I said. "Or I start pulling confessions out of you the hard way. I can feel you're not telling us something crucial, and I'm about ready to physically get it out of you. Don't make me force you to tell the truth."

"I..." He swallowed. "I couldn't find her."

"What?" the Atua was talking erratically, as if the language was a foreign thing his tongue couldn't quite catch.

"Alice," he croaked. "When they took her. I tried to find her. I really did. But I couldn't trace her magic. And when I realized what he'd done to her..." He grabbed fistfuls of hair and started yanking on it. "I..." He trailed off, jaw trembling, eyes darting everywhere but at me.

Dominic stepped forward, and I instinctively raised a hand. "Don't."

"He's lying," Dominic growled. "I can smell it on him."

"No," Samir whispered, wiping his mouth with the back of a trembling hand, dark strands of hair dangling from between his fingers. "I'm not lying. I couldn't find her. But that's not... that's not what I meant." His shoulders sagged. "I'm the reason they found us. I told them where we'd be."

The words were so quiet, they barely registered. But when they did, all the blood left in my body drained to my feet and a loud buzzing started in my ears.

My breath caught.

"What did you just say?" my blood rushed through my veins back up making my whole body tingle and it thundered in my ears.

His hands twitched at his sides. "I told the Council. Or... Frederic, at least. About the location where we would attack. About the safe house, too."

"You what?" Dominic roared, stepping forward like a storm given form.

I slammed a hand into his chest before he could move another inch. "Don't," I hissed. "Let him finish."

Samir's face crumpled. "I didn't think they'd take her!" he cried. "He said if I gave them the location, he'd spare you. That's what he said. You were the one they wanted. You're the threat. The human was never part of the deal."

"You sold us out to save me?" My voice cracked with disbelief.

His eyes met mine, and there it was, raw, pitiful, all-consuming guilt. "Yes," he rasped. "You were going to die,

Brooklyn. I couldn't…I made a promise…I couldn't let that happen. I thought…"

"You thought wrong." Dominic's voice was deadly quiet now. "And you endangered all of us. You betrayed Alice. Rowan. You nearly cost me everything, you dumb mother-fucker. Brooklyn almost died to help Alice."

Samir looked at me again, like there was some absolution he still believed he might receive.

I shook my head. "You don't get to say it was out of loyalty. You don't get to make that call. You chose to trade blood for your own peace of mind so you can keep believing the delusional reality that you are some kind of a savior to me. Disgusting."

He took a step toward me.

"Don't," I said. "Don't you dare come closer." With strength I didn't know I had I pushed down the bile raising up my esophagus.

The weight of Samir's confession didn't hit me like a blow. It didn't shatter me or set my blood roaring with vengeance. Instead, it settled, cold, dense, inevitable…like winter fog rolling in after a sleepless night.

The silence that followed his words was suffocating. I felt it in my teeth, in my lungs, in the hollows behind my ribs where breath once lived freely. I waited for the fury to come. For the instinct to rip him apart for what he had done. For the betrayal he had carved like a brand into the fragile trust we'd once built.

But it didn't come.

What came instead was worse.

Resignation.

Somehow, on a level I hadn't wanted to acknowledge, I'd known. I'd felt the rot spreading under the surface every time Samir averted his eyes, every time he offered silence when we needed truth. I had told myself because I needed to believe it, that he was still different from the Council that had tried to own me, use me, destroy me. That maybe he was the one who had seen past the monsters they painted us to be.

But that belief had always hung by a thread.

Now it snapped, quietly, without ceremony.

I stared at him, and it was like staring at a ruin long since collapsed; Something that had already crumbled, only now I could see it for what it truly was. He didn't look back. Not fully. His eyes were rimmed red, not from tears but from lack of sleep, from whatever devils he'd been wrestling in the dark.

His hand twitched at his side. A nervous tick. His shoulders had slumped inward, like his spine couldn't bear the weight of what he'd done. He was barely holding himself together, as if his very breath was stitched by guilt and unraveling by the second.

"I never meant for it to be her," he said again, his voice fraying. "I was trying to save you."

I blinked at him, stunned by how quiet my own thoughts had become. "No," I said softly. "You were trying to save yourself from watching me die. That's not the same."

Samir's lips parted, but no denial came. His throat worked like he was swallowing glass.

Behind me, the heat radiating off of Dominic might as well have been a furnace. I could feel the storm in him, the coiled tension rippling through his muscles, the unspoken promise of violence vibrating in every breath. But he held still, barely. For me. For the promises I wrung out of him when we were skin to skin and he was vulnerable and raw. I should have been ashamed of the manipulation but I wasn't.

I could've let Dominic tear him apart. I could've said a word, and it would've been done before Samir had time to blink. But I didn't. And what unnerved me more than anything was that I didn't want to.

I didn't want his blood.

Because there was no satisfaction in vengeance when all it confirmed was your worst fear. That no matter how far you ran, no matter how carefully you chose your allies, they still found ways to betray you.

Samir dropped to his knees.

Not dramatically. Not as a plea. But because, I think, his legs simply gave out. He stared at the floor like it could offer him some absolution. Like the cracks in the wood might swallow him whole if he looked hard enough.

"I stayed in my room," he whispered. "Because I couldn't face her. Or you. I heard her screaming in my dreams. I felt it, I felt everything like it was done to me. I knew what they were doing to her although I had no clue where she was. And I knew it was my fault."

Dominic growled low in his throat, a sound that raised every hair on my neck.

I held up a hand again. Not for Samir's sake. For mine.

Samir kept going, almost feverish now. "I went to Frederic because I thought it would be clean. They can have the demons and leave us alone. That I could make a trade, keep you safe, and no one would know. I thought I was in control. But he was never after you...not really. He just wanted a crack in the wall. And I gave it to him."

I took a slow breath, forcing my voice to stay calm. "You were going to give them Echo and Chester? You were supposed to be our friend. You were supposed to protect all of us."

He nodded miserably. "I know."

"So why aren't you dead yet?" Dominic snarled, stepping forward.

"Because I won't let you kill him," I said quietly. "And he is coward enough to be unable to end his own life.

Both men looked at me, stunned for different reasons.

"He is giving this confession because he wants one of us to kill him. I'm not doing this for him," I added, eyes locked on Samir. "You betrayed us, and I hope that guilt eats you alive. But killing you won't bring her suffering back. It won't unmake the mistake. It won't fix a goddamn thing."

Samir closed his eyes. "Then what happens now?"

I straightened, every word a blade between my teeth. My voice laced with my power, more potent, more primal now after my visit with the shaman. "Now? You leave. You vanish. By morning, you and every trace of your existence better be gone from this house. I don't care where you go and you no longer have any right to this place. But if I ever see you again. If I even feel your presence near me or mine...I won't hesitate. No more mercy. No more forgiveness. I will rip you limb from limb with my bare hands, Samir. I mean it."

He nodded, slowly, like it was the one thing he'd been expecting all along.

"I truly am sorry," he whispered.

"I'm not the one who needs your apology," I replied. "But you'll never get to give it to the one person who never deserved suffering from our curse, from any of it."

The silence afterward was immense.

And in that silence, I turned away.

Dominic caught my arm gently, grounding me as the weight of everything sank in. My throat burned, but I didn't cry. I didn't scream. I didn't shatter.

I had no more pieces left to fall.

We left Samir kneeling there in the hallway, the last echo of whatever trust had once existed between us evaporating with every step I took.

I prayed that he felt the sharp pain from each step I took away from him the same way I did.

And I hoped the fucker bled for eternity from it.

Chapter Twenty-Six

ALICE

I barely registered the sound of a door opening before I was already moving. My legs didn't ask for permission; they just flew. Through the corridor, past the creaky floorboard near the pantry, around the corner of the house, my socked feet slipping and sliding over the wooden floors until I saw them.

Brooklyn and Dominic stood in the hallway like shadows turned solid, road-worn and still streaked with dust and tension. But they were real. They were back.

Alive.

I crashed into them like a bowling ball.

"Oomph...Alice...!" Brooklyn staggered under my weight as I hurled myself at her. Dominic, ever the shield, tried to catch us both, but we ended up collapsing backward onto the wall in a mess of limbs and laughter and the kind of relief that's so sharp it borders on pain.

"You're back! You're back!" I cried, voice breaking halfway between sobs and hysteria. "Do you know how mad everyone's been? I mean, I'm so glad you're alive, but what the hell, Brooklyn?! Did you actually try to die again?

Because I swear if you keep doing this, I'm putting you in a cage. A magical, talking cage. With glitter wallpaper and no privacy! A pink one!"

She blinked, wide-eyed, horrified at the picture I painted and still stunned, her mouth half-open.

"I love you, too," she murmured, and that was all it took for another wave of emotion to knock loose in my chest. I was bawling in her arms. Ugly crying with snot and everything.

Dominic groaned beneath us, shifting to sit upright. "Gods, Alice, I think you cracked my rib."

"I think I cracked three," Brooklyn muttered, rubbing her side, but she was smiling, and that was everything.

Echo and Chester came tumbling into the room a moment later, the noise impossible to ignore.

"There you are!" Echo cried, her gaze darting between us. "What happened? We know the shaman helped you. Obviously..." she flicked a wrist at me and I glared at her. "What did you have to do? Did she make you give blood? Sacrifice something? Did she speak in riddles?"

"Slow down," Dominic said, holding up a hand.

Brooklyn winced and sat straighter, pulling herself out from the dogpile. "It's... complicated."

"Oh, come on," Chester grumbled. "We've had nothing but 'complicated' since this whole thing started. At least give us the CliffsNotes."

Brooklyn rubbed her temple and looked at me. "You're okay?"

I nodded, sobering slightly. "I think so. I mean... I feel weird, but not like... cursed-weird. Just tired. Hollow. Like something burned out and left room behind it."

Echo gave a relieved sigh. "At least you don't need to

worry about demonic possession." When we all gaped at her she shrugged. I can sense those."

Then her expression darkened slightly. "Rowan hasn't woken up yet. Still unconscious. He's stable, but... unmoving."

A shadow passed over Brooklyn's face. "We'll figure it out," she said softly. "We have to. The shaman didn't offer any clue about him."

And then, like a switch had been flipped, she harrumphed to herself under her breath.

"Here," she whispered, reaching into her back pocket. "I almost forgot. You'll need these."

She pulled something small and familiar from behind her and held it out to me.

My glasses.

I stared.

"The shaman gave these to you?" Unease started clawing at my insides.

"No," Brooklyn looked at me strangely. "You left them on the front steps. You should be careful, one of us can step on them."

Everything else, voices, light, warmth, it all blurred to nothing. I took them into shaking hands. Scratched, slightly bent. Just as I remembered.

Except I hadn't remembered. Not really. I had convinced myself it was a dream. A hallucination. Some leftover fragment of nightmare tangled in the threads of Frederic's spell.

But it wasn't.

They were real.

She was real.

And so was what happened.

"I thought..." I started, then stopped, trying to get my mouth to work. "I thought I made it up."

The air shifted. All eyes turned to me.

"I wasn't just held imprisoned. I mean, I was, but... there was something else. Someone else." My voice was shaking now, brittle as glass. "Two men dragged me. I remember it. My head was spinning and everything was dark, but I heard them. Arguing."

I looked at Dominic, then Brooklyn. "They said 'she' wanted to see me before the Council got back."

Echo's brow furrowed. "She?"

"I don't know who. But she wasn't part of the Council. I know that. She wasn't one of them. She was something else." I swallowed. "Someone they think they control but they don't."

Chester shifted uncomfortably. "You sure it wasn't just a dream? What?" he snapped when Echo elbowed him. "We have enough shit to deal with without additional boogeyman being added to the mix."

"No," I answered when I could finally speak again. "Because I smelled her. And you can't imagine smells, not like that. She smelled like…" I gagged slightly. "Like lilacs. Like something that should make me feel safe. Protected. Weirdly enough, it did make me feel better when I was around her."

"Safe?" Brooklyn was looking at me with worry scrunching her features and I hated that I had to be the bearer of bad news.

"She smelled very similar to how Dominic smells." I swallowed the lump clogging my throat.

"Another shifter maybe?" Dominic ever the logical one started connecting the dots immediately. But not even he could guess what I actually knew for certain now that I saw.

"A shifter, yes." My hand reached for Brooklyn's, and I grasped her fingers so hard I could hear her bones groan. "A female panther, with eyes like yours."

Echo and Chester inhaled a sharp breath at the same time, their heads snapping toward Dominic who watched me with confusion.

"Eyes like mine?" he parroted. "That's impossible, Alice. Only my family had this color eyes from the panther community. And they are all dead."

My mouth opened to say something, anything really.

No words came out.

The door to the common room cracked open and all of us turned to look at it.

Rowan half stepped out half hung on the door handle, pale as a ghost, dull lifeless sigils flickering erratically all over his skin. Dark circles formed half-moons beneath his eyes that had lost all their color and looked see-through right now.

His gaze locked on Dominic immediately as if he listened to our conversation all along.

"Dominic…" Rowan rasped, his voice thready and raw. "Your…" Coughs raked his body and Dominic jumped up and rushed to catch him when he tilted—just about to fall over.

"My what, Rowan?" Dominic leaned over the witch, pressing his ear to the barely moving lips.

A sharp intake of air was followed by Dominic stumbling back and almost dropping the witch.

"What is it?" Brooklyn was instantly by his side, holding them both steady. "Dominic? What's wrong?"

"My"—his frantic, shocked gaze met hers— "my sister is alive."

Goosebumps covered me from head to toe even though I knew what Rowan would say.

"Frederic has my sister." Dominic whispered.

Rowan shuddered and lost consciousness again.

And me?

I never wanted to see the look in Brooklyn's eyes ever again.

For the first time in my life I was shitless scared of my best friend, my soul sister.

"I'm going to get her back," she said calmly, evenly.

She had never sounded more menacing since I'd known her.

Shit was about to hit the fan.

And that asshat that cursed me?

Frederic was going to regret the day he was born.

Note from the Author

Hello Rebels,

I hope you enjoyed this latest installment in Brooklyn, Alice, and Dominic's stories. I've genuinely missed these characters yapping away inside my head, and I can't wait to hear your thoughts. Thankfully, my health has improved after some challenging moments and surgeries, which means you'll soon have the rest of the sequels in your hands. Believe me, these characters have missed you too. They've become exceptionally chatty lately!

Bringing their emotional journeys, trials, and triumphs to life is incredibly personal for me, and sometimes words fall short of fully expressing the depth of what I'm feeling. That's why your feedback is invaluable. Please leave reviews, reach out in my group, use the contact form on my website, or connect on Facebook. Good or bad, your experiences matter deeply to me and help me grow as a storyteller.

I appreciate each and every one of you. This journey has been remarkable, and it wouldn't have been possible without your incredible support.

With all my love,
Maya

vinci-books.com/restingwitch

Forbidden fruit is sweet... until you take a bite.

I was the dud of my coven—until a failed spell blew up the library and unlocked my magic. In my panic, I tried another one, but instead, I destroyed ancient texts, wrecked half the building, and somehow ended up half-naked in the high priest's office. Now, I'm totally screwed.

Turn the page for a free preview...

Resting Witch Face: Chapter One

Lesson 1: *don't drink and drive.*

No, scratch that. That was for humans. The real lesson was: don't drink and pretend you're something you are not. Like, acting like a badass witch when you have zero magic. Take it from me because it'll destroy your life. Although that was neither here nor there, when it came to me, since I was screwed the day I popped out of my mother's vagina. She died during childbirth, most probably out of disappointment. I kid you not.

I was a dud born in the most powerful bloodline of witches in the world.

How was that for a sap story?

"Hey, buddy," I called out like we're the best of friends. "Get back down here before you hurt yourself and I get blamed for it. What do you say?" The Kishi demon cocked his head and eyed me like I'd lost my mind. Poor schmuck had no idea that ship had sailed years ago.

My foot wobbled in my designer ankle boots when I

took a step forward, and I did an awkward shimmy-wiggle-swan-dive before I regained my balance. It was what happened when you drank one too many Manhattans and answered a call from your coven to deal with a demon selling illegal merchandise.

"Damn you! If I scratch my boots I'm going to skin you alive just to make myself a new pair. I should've just stayed in the damn bar." The racket of a paint can crashing to the floor and rattling around applauded my muttering. It also stabbed my brain, which was pounding like a shifter in heat when a willing body accidentally stumbled in front of his dick. Don't ask me how I know this, because as brutally honest as I am, I'm not going to tell you.

iPhone held in front of me the same way those pompous asses from the Magi Police waved their badges around, I pointed the flashlight right into the creep's eyes. It screeched like a banshee and scattered further into the darkness while I hissed curses at it. Luckily for the demon, none of them would be taking root, because … no magic, duh.

What took my coven mates so long to get to the ware-house? If this was a party they'd be lining up at the door since yesterday. As I looked around the dirty warehouse and the misty odor of congealed blood and decaying bodies made my stomach roll, I couldn't say I blamed them.

The fact that Kishi demons had an attractive human face on the front and a hyena's face on the back of their skull was the least of my problems. Kishi demons used their human face as well as their smooth, luring voice and other tricks to attract unassuming idiots— which I definitely was not, shut it I'm not!—and then they proceeded to eat them with their deformed jaws. That would've been fine and dandy if they kept it under wraps, but this one also made an entire collection of body parts to sell on the magical black market. Quite a smart trick when the market was scarce, but not such a great idea for this guy, because he was dumb enough to get caught. That was *if* I managed to hold him back until the others got to the warehouse. With all the alcohol in my blood system, I got this like a hot potato in a bare hand.

Witches more than other supernaturals paid good money for body parts like the ones stacked all the way to the ceiling in the large building, although nobody liked to talk about it. It was that pink elephant in the room we all ignored. No delusions clouded my mind that my coven would "confiscate" the evidence in the warehouse without blinking an eye. I was basically standing in the middle of a gold mine.

The pentagram tattoo on the side of my forefinger tingled, an annoying reminder when my body thought I should be using magic, as adrenaline raced through my veins. My meat suit never got the memo we were shooting blanks. We were as impotent as Mike, my coven's administrator, according to Sissily.

"Go away witch, or die," the demon cooed, his alluring voice gliding over my skin like a caress and leaving goosebumps in its wake.

"Aww, you actually think I'm a witch." My eyelashes fluttered in his general direction as I stumbled deeper into the warehouse. "How adorable," I deadpanned, a serious expression on my face that froze him in his tracks.

Silence followed.

"Ah, you are the useless one." His face poked through the shadows before he fully emerged to sneer at me from over ten feet up, crouched like a gargoyle on the rafters. "I've heard of you. Pathetic." He dismissed me, as his full lip curled over a row of flat, white teeth.

I hated sneering. It reminded me too much of the looks on my coven mates every time they stared in my direction.

Shaking my head to regain my focus, I swallowed hard when the alcohol tried to come up. All I had to do was keep the hellspawn from escaping until reinforcements arrived, but he was pushing his luck. Even a dud could do that if said dud was not a little drunk and teetering on six-inch heels. I eyed my precious boots for a split second, considering using them as a weapon and chucking them at his head, but I changed my mind. Like hell I would mess up a good pair of designer boots for a stupid demon.

The choice was taken from me when he decided to try a trick called monkey in a circus and sailed through the air, aiming his body straight at me. My phone jerked to follow the arch of the jump, and I had one second of an "oh shit" moment before our bodies collided. Never mind me, my iPhone flew from my fingers, crashed on the concrete floor with a resounding crack, and I heard my silk shirt rip at the shoulder when we tumbled on the dirty concrete floor. I just bought that phone.

I saw red.

Fingers hooked like claws, I went straight for his eyes when he tried to straddle me. Somewhere in the back of my mind I was aware that if he bit me the poison from his kind would kill me in less than an hour, but I had liquid courage, louder than the alarm bells cheering me on. The demon didn't expect me to claw at his eyes, so when my nails made squelching mush out of his eyeballs, his human face roared at me. If I was in the right mind, I would be shaking in my skin. As things were, he resembled a chihuahua nipping at my ankles to my muddled brain. Wretchedly vile breath melted my makeup and I gagged, barely holding back the bile so I didn't puke all over both of us.

"It's called a toothbrush, asshole." I hacked hard enough to cough out a lung while jamming my forearm in his throat to hold back his snapping jaws. The Kishi demon was trying to munch on my face, for fuck's sake. "You should use it, damn you."

Desperate times called for desperate measures, and, as much as it pained me, I had to sacrifice my boots. My leg swung up like a slingshot, caught him on the side of the head, and he went down hard. His head bounced off the concrete, and his skull cracked with enough strength to be heard over the heartbeat in my ears. The air whooshing out of him satisfied my need to hurt him like he hurt my poor blouse. It was also new and cost me an arm and a leg. Using the time I had, I scrambled on my knees, yanked my poor boot off, and nailed him in the neck with the heel. The demon gasped, probably still dazed from the kick, but apart from a few spastic jerks, he didn't attempt to flee. Or move again at all, but that would be semantics.

They might think that was how I found him.

Right.

With a sigh, I dropped on my haunches not a moment too soon before the solid thump of feet came from the entrance behind me. Light jiggled up and down over the stacked shelving from the flashlight the person held, and I looked down my shoulder at the flipping piece of silk that used to be a soft olive color. Dirt, sweat, and dried blood from the scrapes on my upper arm turned the silk some disgusting color of brown. I frowned at the flapping fabric.

"Hands up where I can see them," the owner of the flashlight barked from behind me.

Great. Instead of my coven mates, I had to deal with a human cop. Just my luck for the night, it seemed.

"Do I look dangerous to you?" My head twisted so I

could squint at him over my shoulder, and a bright light stabbed me in the brain like a pickaxe. "Are you trying to blind me on purpose, or is this how you pick up chicks all the time? If they have a flashlight burning their retinas they can't see your ugly face, huh?" Oh yeah, I recognized the voice better than I should've.

"Hazel? What in God's name are you doing here?"

"Getting a tan. You?" I chirped brightly and regretted it when acid filled my mouth. I would never drink again.

"Don't be a smartass. I'm seriously asking what—" His words stopped when he noticed my ripped shirt and one bare foot, and he shuffled closer. I was pretty sure having my skirt bunched up around my hips and flashing the creases of my ass didn't help, either. Goddess, I looked a mess.

"Are you hurt?" His hulking frame kept moving closer, sending my heart to gallop in my chest.

"No, wait." My sudden shout stopped him in his tracks. "Stay there, Davon, you don't want to get bitten." Think Hazel, think.

"Bitten? What the hell, Hazel. Get away from there right now. What's in there?" When a gun cocked, I knew the jig was up. If he saw the demon, there was no doubt in my mind I'd be in more trouble than I already was.

"It's a dog, okay. Stay back because if you spook it, it'll bite me. Then I'll be pissed. Do you want that?" Where the hell was my coven?

"What kind of a dog?" Tone dripping with suspicion, his feet scraped the floor as he cautiously moved closer again. If he saw the Kishi starfishing it, not even my grandmother could cover the mess up.

"You are the one with a flashlight, Davon, so why don't you tell me. I'm not playing games when I tell you to stay back. Look at my face." I added an additional scowl for good measure, shuffling on my knees to hide the Kishi sprawled a couple of feet away, deep enough in the shadows not to be visible for the moment.

"What about it?" I could've laughed at the weariness in that loaded question, but he did stop coming closer.

"Does it say approachable to you right now?"

"It never does," he muttered, and I grinned at him like a fiend. "This is crazy. You don't get to boss me around after you dumped me."

"I already parted with my right boot, and I love these boots. You wanna try the left one? I can nail you in the forehead or in the jingleberries. Your choice," I threatened while internally freaking out. Being a bitch to Davon wouldn't work much longer. It never did. He would do the opposite of what I told him just to spite me. I could feel it.

"Hello," a female voice called from the entrance of the warehouse, and I deflated like a balloon recognizing my best friend Sissily. About freaking time. The demon was dazed, but he wouldn't stay down much longer. And if he woke up with Davon here, I had a nagging feeling my body parts would join those scattered around the warehouse in jars. Courtesy of my grandmother, of course. The demon didn't have shit on her when that witch got pissed.

"Stop right there. Police." Davon pointed his gun and flashlight at Sissily's face. Protecting her poor eyesight with a forearm flung in front of her, she blinked at him as if ready to say something.

"Is this your dog?" I rushed to say before she screwed me over. You never knew what would come out of her mouth. "It might be injured, it almost bit me."

"Hazel ..." Davon started in a warning tone.

"Yeah, oh thank goodness you found him," Sissily

gushed, overdoing it a little, if you asked me. Whatever Davon wanted to say was silenced, thank the goddess.

"If this is your dog, Ma'am, I must report it, I'm afraid. It attacked a civilian, and it's considered dangerous." Davon, the good cop he always was, started reading Sissily her rights while she rolled her eyes.

I sighed, pinching the bridge of my nose.

"Oh, shut up human." Her hand flicked when she had enough of his word vomit, and she zapped him hard enough the poor guy convulsed a long moment before he passed out, the gun and flashlight clattering on the concrete.

Then she turned her blue peepers my way and gave me a once-over. Although her blonde hair was smooth and all in one place, and her pencil suit was sharp enough to cut a finger off, Sissily had no right to grimace at me. Someone should tell her "I bit a rotten lemon" was never a good look on a chick. Just saying.

"If you say a word Im'ma boob punch you." Pushing off the ground, I swayed, and for the second time I failed to glue the ripped silk sleeve together. "Are you alone?" It was improbable, but a girl could hope.

"The others are not far behind me. I had a feeling you'd jump right into this, so I made sure I came before anyone else. What do we have?" She sashayed closer, giving Davon a disgusted look.

"Kishi demon." I glared at the asshole who finally stirred with a groan.

"How do you find yourself in these situations, Hazel?" Ignoring her, I was still messing with the sleeve, so with a sigh, she took her jacket off and handed it to me.

"Thanks." Limping a couple of steps forward, I plucked it from her fingers. "And I wasn't kidding about the boob punch. I'll even twist your nipple until you scream if you don't keep your voice down."

"You do know we're not five anymore, right?"

"What's your point?"

I could tell she had so much to say just by the tightening of the tendons on her neck. Her throat worked, her mouth opening and closing until she gave up and shook her head.

Yeah, exactly my sentiments.

"Where's your other boot?" She followed the elaborate swirl of my finger until it pointed at the demon. My beautiful, precious boot was sticking out of his throat, covered in black blood and gore. Then she arched an eyebrow, which should've looked stupid on anyone except me, but on Sissily everything looked good. If she wasn't my best friend and if I had magic, I would've hexed her with warts. I hoped the girl knew how lucky she was that I loved her like a sister. What surprised me more was she loved me back the same, even though I was an asshole. At least most of the time.

"I've always told you fashion is a weapon if you learn how to use it. Did you believe me? Of course you didn't." My smirk earned me a twitch of her mouth. If anyone knew Sissily they'd know it for the huge win that was. She never smiled on a job.

"Danika is going to lose her shit." We both shivered at that.

As if saying the name conjured her, my grandmother's power preceded her presence, filling the warehouse with magic and saturating the air with the strong scent of ozone.

"Hazel Byrne." I flinched when my name echoed in the silent building, and Sissily copied me sympathetically. "Show your face this instant." My grandmother swooped in like a hungry vulture honing-in on a roadkill.

Me. I was the roadkill.

Thankfully, the lights came on inside the building, blinding me momentarily as thumps of many feet scattered throughout the warehouse. Our coven mates spread around the vast space like ants. I blinked like an idiot a few times until my vision cleared, and that was when I saw the look on her face. Cold, emerald eyes sharp enough to cut a diamond rolled over me from head to toe, assessing and judging while telling me she found me lacking in many ways. I gulped and tugged Sissily's jacket closer. Then Danika's unreadable gaze fell on Davon, who took a lesson from the Kishi demon and was starfishing it in the middle of the damn place. She stilled at the sight of a human cop and stabbed me with a glare afterwards.

"That was Sissily, not me." The words burst from me so fast I almost spit on my lower lip.

"Snitch," my best friend hissed, but her chin jutted out and she stepped closer to me.

"Every bitch for herself, remember?" I mumbled behind my hand when I raised it to wipe my mouth in case I was still drooling. Those Manhattans were buzzing in my head like a cloud of bees and making my tongue too thick for my mouth while I swayed where I stood. Oh boy was I screwed.

Sissily snorted but coughed to cover it up. Her reaction earned me a disapproving look from my grandmother, which I felt all the way to my soul. The woman saw everything no matter how hard I tried to hide it, and her hearing was better than a vampire's. I didn't have to guess because I *knew* she heard us.

I was the best fighter they had in our coven. Hand-to-hand or weapon combat, I could take them all down, and that included our high priest. But thanks to my lack of magic, I somehow always ended up looked down on, especially by Danika Byrne. Even when I did get the job done.

One demon stabbed in the throat with a designer boot, case and point.

"We will speak back at the coven." With flare, she spun on her heel, her long dress billowing behind her as she stormed out of the warehouse and left me grinding my teeth.

"Let's go." Linking her hand through mine, Sissily tugged me along with her because she probably assumed I would run. And honestly, I thought about it for like two point five seconds. It was pointless since everything I had was in the house I shared with my grandmother, but it sure was tempting. I wobble-limped alongside Sissily, glancing at my coven mates as they packed everything, including the Kishi demon I apprehended.

"She will chill out by the time we get back." My best friend gnawed on her lower lip, not believing her own assurances.

"I don't care." My shrug didn't fool her since I was patting my hair to smooth it and probably looked constipated just thinking about facing my grandmother behind closed doors.

Because Danika Byrnes never chilled. Like ever. My grandmother was born with a stick so far up her ass the goddess herself couldn't find it if she tried.

She was going to hand my ass to me, and I had no other choice but to take whatever she dished out. A sinking suspicion that it would involve cleaning churned in my stomach right beside the booze.

There was a first time for everything, though. She might've grown a heart in the last twelve hours. Or took it from some random jar and shoved it in her chest. My head tilted to the side, I contemplated it for a second.

One look at my grandmother's disappearing form, with

those stiff shoulders and that head held high, killed that hope. There was no escaping a punishment.

With a groan, I followed my best friend into the belly of the beast.

The whole way back to the coven, I kept trying to picture my eyeballs floating in a jar on top of my grandmother's desk.

They were a nice shade of golden honey, if I did say so myself. I'd have them in a jar too if I didn't need them.

Resting Witch Face: Chapter Two

The Gatekeeper's coven was located dab smack in the middle of Cleveland, of all places. The temple walls stretched high toward the sky like the open mouths of baby birds waiting for a worm to fall into their gaping maws. A domed ceiling made of glass, to better see the full moon each month, covered almost half the block. Made out of black stone, the building looked menacing, and the three keys − a symbol representing Hecate- painted in blood red above the tall double doors of the entrance stood out stark against it. Since it was late at night, magical flames were shooting seven feet tall on each side of the stars leading to it, casting it in an eerie-hellish hue. No wonder humans gave us a wide berth.

Pausing at the bottom of the marble steps that would lead me inside, I glanced up and down the street. An urge to book it down the sidewalk and find a place to hide for a day or two was very tempting. However, with only one boot and still mostly drunk, there was no way I could outrun Sissily.

She might sympathize with me, but she was a stickler for the rules, and she was smart enough not to want to anger Danika, unlike me. I had no doubt she'd tackle me and drag me kicking and screaming inside by the hair. She did that once in middle school when I didn't want to go back inside with her after lunch break. The humans mulling around would be no help, either. Ever since we came out of the closet, so to speak, they gawked like we were circus freaks but wouldn't come closer than a few feet, as if magic was contagious and they might get infected. I wish it was.

There were exceptions like Davon the cop, but those were few and far between. We were "the others," and unless they needed help, humans wanted nothing to do with us. At least there were no pitchforks or burnings at the stake involved, so not bad I guessed. That was why my coven was very strict. The government told us we were all good to live among humans as long as no problems came up by *any* supernatural being, not just us. So, the high priest and my grandmother—to be honest it was probably all her because the priest was practically a mute when around her—decided we would boss the supernatural world around. The magi police force was just a front for posturing. We were the ones that got down and dirty. And destroyed perfectly new pairs of designer boots in the process, I'd like to add.

Sissily took my elbow and waddled me up the steps when I took too long to move. Chewing on the inside of my mouth, I allowed my fear to choke me until I reached the double doors, and then I squared my shoulders. Whatever issues I had would be left at the door. No one needed to know my shit. It was none of their business, anyway.

The inside of the building was also painted black, with a hallway like one long intestine twisting around offices, ritual rooms, guest reception halls, and the library, of course. Our pride and joy, with knowledge gathered for generation after generation by magical families. It was the largest collection in the world, and the love of my grandmother's life. I personally used it to hide from idiots when they got annoying, or to pretend I was busy when we had a ritual scheduled. If I was busy, I couldn't participate and see all the pitying looks or sneers thrown my way.

"You ready?" Sissily mumbled under her breath and dragged me out of my spinning thoughts.

"No."

"Hazel."

"Why does everyone think saying my name will help anything?" I jerked my elbow out of her pinching hold and tugged hard on the borrowed jacket to straighten it. My balance went sideways, and I pitched forward, but she tugged me back before I face planted. "Let me tell you, it does nothing but piss me off and feed my anxiety. I know what my name is. I've had it my whole life, thank you very much."

"You're stalling."

"No." I gasped dramatically. "What in the world gave you that idea?" Sissily rolled her blue peepers at me. "I really don't want to go in. I might puke all over her desk."

"You're so stupid." She snickered and bumped my shoulder. For her sake, my lips pulled to the side in a pathetic attempt at a smile.

With a sigh, I continued my impersonation of Quasimodo hobbling down the hall on one high-heeled boot and one bare foot, darting glances at the candelabras lining the walls. Black pillar candles burned in clusters with blue flames, the magical fire standing straight without a crackle or a flicker. They always looked like a painting that gave off light to me, and it didn't matter how many times I saw them.

"They are expecting you." We hadn't fully rounded the corner yet, but Mike made sure to shout it like he was playing bingo and just won. He leered at Sissily, but as soon as he met my glare, his head ducked down so fast he almost headbutted the desk.

"I see you didn't take your meds today, Mike?" I jabbed him conversationally, and Sissily snorted.

"What? Yes, I did." His face snapped up and reddened like a tomato. "Hey, I don't take medication."

I pursed my lips, eyeing him and pretending like I didn't believe him.

Something told me if I kept looking at him his head might explode. I was willing to test that theory, but I felt Danika's magic reaching, plus Sissily nudged me to get moving.

"Maybe you should." My suggestion to the creep in passing left him sneering. "Meds won't grow your brain, but it'll help with your complexion."

We left him stuttering and talking to himself about bitches and the goddess knew what other fairy tales he told himself. After he dared to treat my best friend like she was his personal punching bag while she dated him, I made it my business to mess him up every chance I had. I was pretty sure he cast a protection spell around himself specifically against me so I couldn't physically harm him. Good thing, too, because I didn't trust myself not to fillet him like a fish.

I flung the door open without a knock and hobble-hopped inside my grandmother's office with Sissily nipping on my heels. Stopping in my tracks, I took in the large, ornate-oak desk Danika Byrne sat ramrod straight behind. High Priest Shadowblood was behind her right shoulder, his face pinched so tight it looked like he was trying not to fart. His slicked dark hair, long, thin nose, and pointed chin brought the image of a crow perched on my grandmother's shoulder to my mind every time he did that, although I never dared mention it. But it wasn't those two that made me freeze with one foot in the air and one hand gripping the doorknob.

No, it was the third person in the room just to the left of Danika. In his late twenties to mid-thirties, he was a face I'd never seen before between these walls. His blond hair was shaved close to his skull on the sides, with the top left longer to drape over his forehead in a wave. Eyes the color of melted chocolate flicked my way when I opened the door, and they widened in interest—not enough to be obvious, but since I was staring at him like an idiot, I noticed. A square jaw and a nose with a slight bump at the bridge like it had been broken a time or two framed full lips more suitable to a woman than someone like him. Wide shoulders stretched his indigo button-down shirt, which was tucked into the waistband of dark slacks that emphasized his narrow waist and muscular body. I gawked for less than five seconds, but it was enough for one corner of his mouth to twitch. That little quirk snapped me out of my daze.

Spinning around, I bolted out of the office and plowed Sissily down. She would've fallen on her ass if I didn't catch her by the arm and drag her back out with me. The door closed behind us with a loud thump when I bodily carried her to the desk where Mike was still muttering curses at me.

"Give me your shoes." My best friend squeaked when I plopped her ass on the desk.

"What? Why?"

"Shoes woman. Now." My hand was wiggling in her face to show my urgency. "Questions later."

I yanked them off her feet myself because I had no time to explain why having shoes instead of one boot—regardless of how pretty said boot may look—was so important. Lifting her leg up pushed Sissily until she was leaning on her hands, and if I wasn't in a hurry I would've chortled at Mike's face. Poor schmuck almost swallowed his tongue when he received a face full of a ponytail, and his saucerlike eyes told me he didn't miss Sissily's boobs sticking up from her arched back. I even stabbed her foot in my one boot because I was a good friend like that, and then I was yanking her along with me to enter the office for the second time. She'd probably replace my shampoo with glue to pay me back for this, but I'd deal with it later.

When I stepped back inside the office, my grandmother arched an eyebrow not looking very pleased, which I ignored, of course. Being the nice little witch I was, I waited for Sissily to limp inside before I closed the door and guided her to the closest chair. Her blue eyes were spitting daggers at me the whole time. As Sissily dropped on the uncomfortable chair, I went as far as petting her head like a puppy that did potty, ignoring her glare the entire time. Then, I turned and beamed at everyone in the room, giving my grandmother a pointed look towards blondie that said help a girl out but I had a feeling my plea fell on deaf ears.

"Hazel, what happened tonight?" Danika Byrne got down to business, stapling her fingers under her chin and leaning her forearms heavily on the desk. If looks could kill, Sissily would be reading my obituary right now.

Smile frozen on my face to flash my pearly whites, I

widened my eyes at her. "What?" My lips didn't move as I pushed the question through my teeth. My best friend groaned from the side.

"What in the goddess's name is wrong with you?" I swore lightning flashed in Danika's emerald eyes. "Are you hurt? Did the demon do anything to you?"

"We don't discuss coven business in front of strangers, Dani—I mean, Ma'am. Grandmother," I added that last bit lamely as an afterthought, and the thunderous expression twisting her features told me she didn't miss it.

"River Blackman is an apprentice of our high priest, Hazel." She looked down her nose at me like I was supposed to be psychic and guess who was who around here without introduction. "There are no strangers."

Wait, what?

"You can have your shoes back." With a groan, I turned to Sissily and started tugging the shoes off my feet. I shoved them in her face, and she recoiled as if I'd thrown snakes at her.

"I don't want them." She attempted to slap my hands away with a mortified look on her face, but I was very persistent when I needed to be.

"Well, you're having them." I jabbed them at her again. "Give me my boot."

"What in the world is going on?" We all ignored the high priest when he mumbled at no one in particular, sounding perplexed.

"You are aware that you are nuts, right?" Sissily muttered under her breath, but she tugged her shoes on, and I yanked the one boot over my foot.

"Of course. I'm an asshole, Sissily, but I'm not stupid." She blinked at my incredulous tone, but I was already turning toward the rest of the people in the room.

A muscle twitched under my grandmother's eye.

"When the call came for the demon, everyone that answered was at least twenty minutes away. Everyone in this room knows they are sneaky and fast." I figured I'd get it over with. "I was closest to the demon, so I answered the call and made sure he didn't escape. Long story short, he is in our hands and the warehouse ransacked ..." Danika's scowl was a creature all on its own. "I'm sure you don't want to hear my internal debate about sacrificing my new boots so he didn't get away, Grandmother."

Grating on my nerves was the fact that River's eyes were dancing with suppressed humor. *Laugh it up, asshole, because I'll make you cry soon enough.* I wasn't sure he read the message I shot his way through my narrowed gaze, but he couldn't say he wasn't warned. Being a dud was a sure thing to get you bullied in a coven full of powerful witches, so instead of dealing with that, I became a master at cracking their noses with my fist. The blondie wouldn't know what hit him.

"I do want to hear every detail there is. Starting with what possessed you to go there in the first place. Fighting a demon without magic is unacceptable." If she noticed my flinch, she didn't show it. "He could've killed the last of the Byrne line, you insolent girl."

"How's this for a recap, Danika?" I snarled. The gasp from Shadowblood sounded scandalized when I slapped both hands on her desk and leaned forward so we were at eye level. "I can kick any demon's ass, including every idiot you have inside this coven, in six-inch heels, without breaking a sweat, and with my arms tied behind my back. I showed up at the warehouse, cracked the demon's head on the concrete like a melon, then I stabbed him with my new boot. Which you owe me a new pair, plus an iPhone, just so you know. Then the rest of you waltzed into posture with your magic and clean up the place. That good enough of an explanation for you?"

"How dare you speak like that?" High Priest Shadowblood stuttered, his neck elongating as he tucked his chin in. "You are not a savage, young lady."

"Aren't I, though?"

"Show respect to your grandmother," he snapped.

"You got one thing right, pops." My empty stare flicked his way, and he took an involuntary step back. If they don't string me from the roof tonight, I'm honestly never drinking again. "*My* grandmother, and I'm doing exactly what she taught me. To quote her, 'you treat people the way they treat you.' So, I will talk to her however damn well I please. In this case, I'm showing her the same respect she gave me." I believe Shadowblood was about to have an aneurism.

"Hazel," Danika leaned back in her chair on a sigh, all fight draining out of her. "I wasn't trying to insult you because you have no magic."

For an old witch, barely any lines were visible on her beautiful face. She might be a stick-up-the-ass nag, but no one could dispute the fact she still turned heads. Midnight blue hair spilled around her face like a waterfall, bringing attention to her alabaster skin and piercing emerald eyes. Tall for a woman, she was curvy where it counted, but most admirable of all was her presence. When Danika Byrne walked into a room, you knew it even if your back was turned.

"No, you were complimenting me on a job well done." With one last stare at Shadowblood, I pushed off the desk. "If we are done here, I need a shower. I can smell the Kishi demon on my skin."

"I need you to promise me—"

"I will not step foot anywhere where your precious

witches with magic need to go." My smile could cut glass when I looked at her over my shoulder. "I'll just stand back and look pretty."

"You are not replaceable, Miss Byrne——" Shadowblood started, but I cut him off.

"No, I'm to be kept as a broodmare, High Priest Shadowblood. I'm aware." That got the reaction I expected from my grandmother.

"For the next week, you will be cleaning the library, Hazel," Danika snapped and stood to her full height, which was a couple of inches higher than mine. She did it on purpose so I had to look up at her. *Nice power play, Grandma.* "And the ritual room, too, until I say that you are done. Am I clear?"

"Crystal." I dared a glance at River, but with his hands clasped at the small of his back, he was frowning at his boots. *Welcome to the Gatekeeper's Coven, blondie, this is how we treat family.* The guy hasn't done anything to me, but just seeing him standing behind that desk with Danika and Shadowblood put him in my shit bucket, too.

"Let's go," I called out to my best friend, who was in the office for moral support more than anything else.

We almost made it out the door. Almost.

"Sissily, you'll join Hazel in her tasks." My grandmother was already back in her chair and had turned to say something to River Blackman, a blunt dismissal of us if ever I saw one.

We spilled out of the office without another word. "Why do I pay every time you get into trouble, little jerk?"

"Because you are the only one that can call me that and live, big jerk." I threaded my arm through hers, leaning against her for support.

"True." She sighed and placed her head on my shoulder. "On a good note, not even you can get in trouble inside a library."

Lesson 2: *never tempt fate.*

That bitch bit.

Grab your copy...
vinci-books.com/restingwitch

About the Author

Maya Daniels, USA Today Bestselling and multi-award-winning supernatural suspense author, is a fun-loving woman with many talents.

She traveled the world, gaining life experiences that helped her career as an investigative journalist, as well as her storytelling. Maya writes compelling tales of magic, mythical creatures, loyalty, and life-changing friendships with snarky female characters—much like herself.

Her travels have taken her to Europe, Africa, Asia, Australia, and America. Born with her feet in motion, she currently resides in Ohio, spinning her next epic story that you will not want to put down.

Her biggest 'sins' are her love of chocolate and coffee—through an IV drip! One to never sit still, Maya practices Reiki healing, different types of martial arts, reads about the arcane, talks to furry creatures more than humans, picks up a sledgehammer for home improvement, and travels with her fated mate, seeking her own adventures.